Raves For the Crime Novels of ROBERT TERRALL!

"A succession of explosive amusements, breathless, harassed, handsomely diverting."
—*New York Herald Tribune*

"Ben Gates proves himself a much better than average private eye...refreshingly unhackneyed, and the telling is crisp and well paced."
—*The New York Times*

"Best...thriller since Cain's 'Double Indemnity.' Don't miss it!"
—*King Features Syndicate*

"A riotous flurry of extortion [and] impersonations."
—*Publishers Weekly*

"Fast-moving adventure...filled with slick skullduggery."
—*New York Post*

"Ingenious...Blue-chip humor...Cheerful chicanery."
—*Kirkus Reviews*

"Imaginative...Hair-r...
—*Clevelan...*

D1431638

"Come on in," a girl's voice called. "It's not locked." I went in. She was up on a stepladder painting a wall yellow.

"Why, Mr. Gates," she said. "This is an honor."

She came down the ladder. Her hair was two shades of light brown. She was in her early twenties, and if she wasn't married already I didn't think she would stay unmarried long.

"Painting," she said unnecessarily. "How's the private detective business?"

"About the same. How did you know my name was Gates?"

"The girls were talking about you last night. Most of us hadn't ever seen a real live private detective, and we thought you were pretty stimulating. You know how girls are?"

"Within limits." I took out a cigar and began peeling off the cellophane. "What I wanted to ask you—"

"Come on in and sit down," she said.

I followed her through an open arch and sat on a couch. She settled on a sort of hassock, tucking one foot under her. She had fewer buttons on her shirt than I had thought at first. Even with close scrutiny, and this is a matter which I like to give close scrutiny, I could only count one.

I bit the end off the cigar. "Do you always put on make-up this early, even when you're not expecting anybody?"

She gave a little laugh. "All right, I knew you were coming. They want me to watch out, because you're supposed to be pretty shifty."

She got up for a cigarette. The cigarettes were on a low table in front of the couch. She had to bend over, and the shirt responded to the pull of gravity. The final button was hanging by a thread. She shifted position, and the crucial button came off with a pop.

"Just as I suspected," I said. "You're a girl."

She was smiling. "Don't you like girls?"

That was when a police car came to a noisy halt in front of the house and two uniformed troopers jumped out...

Kill Now,
PAY LATER

by **Robert Terrall**

A HARD CASE CRIME NOVEL

A HARD CASE CRIME BOOK
(HCC-035)
September 2007

Published by

Dorchester Publishing Co., Inc.
200 Madison Avenue
New York, NY 10016

in collaboration with Winterfall LLC

ISBN 0-8439-5775-1
ISBN-13 978-0-8439-5775-4

Cover design by Cooley Design Lab

Typeset by Swordsmith Productions

The name "Hard Case Crime" and the Hard Case Crime logo
are trademarks of Winterfall LLC. Hard Case Crime books are
selected and edited by Charles Ardai.

Printed in the United States of America

Visit us on the web at www.HardCaseCrime.com

KILL NOW, PAY LATER

Chapter 1

The bride wore a bouffant gown of off-white silk taffeta with a fitted bodice of Alençon lace. The groom wore striped pants, a carnation and a look of bitter regret. As for me, Ben Gates, I was wearing my .38 in a shoulder rig inside my best dacron and worsted. But I wasn't a guest. Most of the wedding receptions I go to socially take place in bar-and-grills. An insurance company had hired me to come to this one and make sure that nobody went home with any of the wedding presents.

A striped marquee had been pitched on the lawn. The bride's father, the president of a big pharmaceutical company and obviously loaded, had supplied thirty cases of imported champagne and another fifty of domestic, to be broached when the guests were too far along to care about the difference. From the library, where I was stationed, the popping of corks sounded like target practice on a 4.2 mortar range. At dusk the Japanese lanterns hanging from the edge of the marquee were turned on. The cars thinned out, the State Trooper went off duty, only a hard core of serious drinkers remained. I continued to get visitors from time to time, but most of them were trying to find a bathroom. One of the maids, a small fair-haired girl who looked pleasantly warm inside her black uniform, brought me a pot of coffee and a platter of sandwiches from the buffet. I considered this thoughtful of somebody. She put her tray down in a space I cleared for her on the coffee table. Her uniform was perhaps a half size too large, and she was doing a certain amount of moving around inside it. We exchanged some boy-girl conversation, as one non-guest to another, and I asked her when she was due to go off. Eleven-thirty, she said, which I considered an interesting coincidence. I was due to go off at eleven-thirty myself.

The sandwiches were small, oddly shaped and a little soggy. I ate them all, down to the last anchovy and the last globule of caviar. The coffee was hot and strong. I poured a second cup and lighted a cigar. A piano was playing somewhere in the house, and a pick-up vocal group was singing dirty limericks. The steady popping of corks outside had made me edgy, but I was finally beginning to think that it might turn out to be an uneventful evening. I try not to have that kind of thoughts, because I always have them just before the trouble starts.

Sure enough, a blonde in a blue dress was poking in at me from the doorway.

"So here's where they're hiding the wedding presents," she said.

She had a glass in one hand, a champagne bottle in the other. As she came into the room I saw that she was barefoot. I didn't need to take her blood count to know she had enough little bubbles inside her to lift her off the floor, like those speedboats which travel on a cushion of foam. I had seen the same blue dress on other girls that afternoon, which probably meant she was one of the bridesmaids. It was a demure dress, but there was nothing demure about what was inside it. The dress had been engineered to be worn with high heels, and the shock-waves set up an interesting play of movement, chiefly in an up-and-down direction, but accompanied by a small amount of sway. Her lipstick was slightly crooked.

I set my coffee cup on the arm of the leather sofa.

"Don't get up," she said as I got up. "Just browsing."

The most valuable presents were displayed on a big refectory table in the center of the room, with the overflow on two trestle tables against the walls. I rotated my cigar to get it burning evenly, not looking at the girl directly as she made a clockwise circuit of the main table. She stopped in front of a tea service of heavy silver to finish the champagne in her glass, holding the stem between her middle fingers in what as far as I know may be the approved grip. She leaned forward to read a card propped against the teapot. Her nose wrinkled.

"Pretty awful, isn't it? But that uncle lives in Texas, so they can take it back to Tiffany's and trade it in for some salad forks."

She rode the bubbles around the table. "Excuse me. They already have salad forks."

A little further she said, "They *certainly* have salad forks."

Suddenly she gave a little cry, put down the bottle and the glass and picked up a bracelet. "The girls have been gossiping about this one."

There was a prominent notice directly in front of her, requesting guests not to handle the presents, but I didn't bother to point it out. I drifted to the right, getting between her and the door. She fastened the bracelet on her wrist and held it up.

"Now *that* is gorgeous," she said with approval. "What's your name?"

When I didn't answer she looked at me. "You."

"Ben Gates," I said without taking the cigar out of my mouth.

"Who do you work for, the insurance company?"

"Today I do," I said. "I'm a private detective. They sent me out to keep good-looking blondes from helping themselves to the diamond bracelets."

She laughed. "The trouble with you is, you're sober."

"That's one of the rules."

As she came around the corner of the table toward me, I felt an unreasonable flicker of alarm. She couldn't have weighed more than one-ten stripped, in itself an interesting thought. But I was getting a good look at her eyes for the first time. She wasn't a solemn drunk. She was one of the wild ones. She was quiet enough at the moment, but it was the quiet of an unexploded torpedo.

I started counting backward from ten.

"Let me hold this," she said.

She took the cigar out of my mouth before I could do anything to stop her. We were as close as we could get without colliding and she kept on coming. Her free hand glanced off my chest and slid up around my neck. Without her shoes on, the top of her head was on a level with my chin, but she didn't let that bother her. She came up me like a caterpillar climbing a wall. I didn't help her, except insofar as the wall can be said to help the caterpillar.

Her lips were open, and I tasted champagne. I'm not enough of an expert on champagne to know if it was domestic or imported. I took a backward step. She stayed with me, and we were now in position to go into the juvenile-delinquent dance known as the fish. Contact was total, and I felt a strong pressure against my eyeballs. It wasn't painful. It wasn't even exactly unpleasant. It was just there, and it seemed out of proportion. She shouldn't have been affecting me that much.

She pushed off. If she had waited a fraction of a second longer we would have gone over backward.

"Weddings always make me feel amorous," she said. "I start kissing people."

"Didn't the bracelet have anything to do with it?"

"Maybe a little." She studied me as though I had just blown in from extra-galactic space. "Without the cigar, you know you look quite nice? Sort of rugged. You've been around, haven't you?"

"Here and there," I said.

She tapped the ash off the cigar elaborately, and put the cigar in her mouth. She didn't quite succeed in carrying it off. She gave a single sharp cough, laughed and handed it back. The pressure on my eyeballs, whatever it was, had relaxed.

"Now suppose you take off the bracelet," I said.

"Oh, Ben," she said, disappointed in me. "You can't

really think I expected to accomplish anything with just one kiss? But you've heard of buying things on installments. That was the down payment."

She found the champagne bottle. "If I got another glass would you join me?"

"I just had some," I said.

She laughed again. "That wasn't nearly enough. I want you to get so drunk you'll forget I'm wearing somebody else's bracelet."

She sipped at her champagne, using the same back-hand grip. She kept looking at me and I had a feeling she was laughing. I couldn't help that. I stayed between her and the door, hoping that I looked incorruptible.

"If you change your mind about the champagne," she said, "I'll let you use my glass."

She sat down in one of the leather armchairs, stretching her feet out in front of her. Her legs were clearly outlined under the blue dress, from the painted toes all the way up. She lifted her wrist and tilted it slightly, to get a glint from the diamonds.

"Are you going to wrestle me for it?"

"I hope not," I said.

"And first you'd have to catch me," she went on. "I can move fast when I have to. Maybe I can trip you up and get out the door. I know my way around the house. You'd never find me."

"All I'd have to do is ask for the wedding picture," I said. "The big one, including the bridesmaids. I don't want to get your hopes up by paying you any compliments, but I think I'd recognize you."

"Then it would be your word against mine, right?"

I was beginning to get the same odd fuzziness I had felt when her tongue was in my mouth. "But they'd believe me."

She sighed. "I suppose you're right. But I wish it was mine! It makes me feel—completely different. I just had a fight with somebody, not that you'd be interested. I looked all over for a certain son of a bitch, and I found him in the back seat of the family Cadillac with one of my fellow bridesmaids. Of course we're wearing the same color dress today, and maybe he was confused. Don't be so square, Ben. Let me keep it." She looked at me seriously, as though she were asking for something of no value, like my autograph. "What would happen if one tiny little bracelet was missing when you turn in the rest of the stuff?"

"First they'd rip off my fingernails," I said. "Then they'd put me in the hole for six months on bread and water. After that they wouldn't give me any business. They have an association. They'd put the word around —when you need somebody, don't call Gates, because he's a man who gives away bracelets."

I locked the door to the hall and put the key in my pocket. She watched warily.

"Now we start chasing each other?"

"Not yet," I said. "I'm supposed to be able to handle a little thing like this without working up a sweat. As soon as I found out they had eighty cases of champagne for five hundred people, I called New York and talked them into sending out another man. His name's

Irving Davidson, and he played pro football after college. Between the two of us we should be able to take off that bracelet."

"It sounds like fun," she said.

"It would be a lot simpler to take it off yourself."

She lifted the champagne glass and smiled at me without replying. There was a tiny point of light in each eye, like a reflection from the diamonds. I went to the window. I heard a shout outside, followed by a burst of feminine laughter. The mixed chorus, wearying of "Sweet Violets," had moved along to "Show Me the Way to Go Home." I, too, would have liked to be shown that way. I was tired and I wanted to go to bed.

I saw Davidson at the far end of the terrace, looking down at the parked cars. A girl in a white dress was talking to him eagerly. Davidson is easily the best-looking private investigator in New York, and girls have difficulty keeping their hands off him. With me and girls, it's usually the other way around.

I rapped on the glass with a half dollar. He heard it and turned.

"All right," the girl said behind me. "I won't make any more trouble. Here."

She was standing. She put down her glass and began picking at the unfamiliar clasp of the bracelet.

"I like competent men," she said, "and, dear God, do I need one right now. Maybe I could hire you. How would I—"

"It's easy," I said. "I'm in the Manhattan book. If you didn't get my name the first time, it's Gates."

"But if you don't let me keep this bracelet, how can I pay your fee?"

Somebody rattled the doorknob. A man's voice called, "Shelley? Shelley?"

"Christ!" she said. The little flares of excitement came back to her eyes. "I've just had the most marvelous idea! Ben—listen. That's my boy. Do me a favor! You don't have to say anything, just hold still and look guilty. But you're too neat. He won't think we've been playing doctor in here unless you're a little more tousled."

She yanked at my tie, pulling me in against her, and put some more lipstick near my mouth. I stepped back, knocking over her glass. Champagne splashed on my coat.

"That's better," she said.

There was a furious knocking at the door. "Shelley!" the voice shouted. "I can hear you whispering! I know you're in there. Open this goddam door before I kick it down!"

I straightened my tie, feeling more and more like the one man at this party on the wagon. I tried to rub off some of the lipstick, but the doorknob was being rattled so furiously that there was a real danger it would be pulled off the door. I used the key. As the bolt cleared, a powerfully built young man knocked the door out of my hands. This was Richardson Pope, Jr., the bride's brother. He had changed out of his formal clothes into a checked jacket and chinos. His face was flushed with champagne and suspicion.

"Chauffeurs, golf pros!" he shouted at the girl. "What taste!"

"Do you know Mr. Gates?" she said coolly.

He seized her shoulders. "You think you can make a fool of me at my sister's wedding, do you? In front of my friends?"

"Friends?" she asked.

"All right, boys and girls, let's cut it out," I said without much conviction.

Davidson walked in. "Need me, Ben?"

Damn right I needed him. I needed any help I could get. Suddenly it was all I could do to keep my eyes open. I was riding a revolving seesaw, going slowly up and down and around, all at the same time. I was getting some peculiar reactions, considering that among all the champagne drinkers I had had nothing to drink but a single cup of coffee. And then it hit me. The coffee had been slightly bitter. I had thought the bitterness was an aftertaste from the fish-spread or the caviar. But if—

"Let go of me," Shelley was saying reasonably.

Pope tightened his grip. "You'd do it with anybody, wouldn't you?" he said, his face close to hers. "You're the one needs analyzing, not me. They have a word for your trouble, and I'll tell you what it is. *Nymphomania!*"

Reaching behind her, she picked a silver cream pitcher off the table and hit him with it. Pope staggered back, his hand going to his forehead.

I reached for her arm and she whirled on me. The waiting violence I had seen back of her eyes was out in the open. She struck at my face with her fingernails.

I had plenty of time to get out of the way, but my responses were slow. It was like being clawed with a blueberry rake.

"With anybody!" Pope yelled again. "And when I think I was almost dumb enough to marry you!"

Shelley laughed harshly. "I thought that had been canceled."

"It is now, by God! It is now!"

"But don't ask me to give back the ring," she said. "I may need to raise some money on it."

Davidson was holding Pope from behind. The boy's mouth worked, and I saw tears in his eyes.

"A detective!" he said. "Shell, I don't see how you could do it."

"Oh, you hypocrite," she said scornfully. "If there's one thing in the world I can't stand, it's hypocrisy. How about my good friend Tina Hare in the back of the Cadillac?"

"We were just—"

"You were just!" Shelley said. "I know how much you were just. And while we're on the subject of adolescent love-play, how about last Saturday? I don't suppose you went visiting in White Plains at one o'clock in the morning?"

Pope lowered his head, and stood absolutely still. *"You followed me?"*

"Oh, yes."

"I'll kill you," he said, and then shouted, "I'll kill you!"

"Why don't you?" she cried. "Haven't you had enough practice?"

I wasn't getting much of this. The seesaw was doing its best to throw me. The voices cut in and out, as though they came from a TV set with a poor connection.

It takes two sober men to hold one determined drunk, and Pope broke away from Davidson. Shelley jerked her head back so his fist didn't land solidly, but it succeeded in knocking her down.

"Dick?" a woman's voice said from the doorway. "Is everything all right, dear?"

I couldn't speak for anybody else, but things were definitely not all right with me. The woman's face went out of focus. I bore down hard and brought it back. She was enormously fat and loaded with jewels, like the wife of a slum landlord in an old-fashioned radical cartoon. Her face was powdered chalk-white, with little red features painted on it. Her fingers were crowded with rings, most of them too tight, and her necklace must have been worth its weight in thousand-dollar bills. The jewelry made a very strong statement, but without it, in spite of her immense bulk, she would have seemed dazed and uncertain.

"I want to go up," she said in a little girl's voice. "And Dickie-bird, you did promise you wouldn't have any more to drink."

The boy's tension drained away. "Oh, Jesus, mother."

I reached for the corner of the table, but it was gone by the time my hand got there. The walls had begun to change places.

"Get them out of here, Irving," I said.

He gave me a quick look. "What's that, Ben?"

"Somebody slugged the goddam coffee."

"Somebody what?"

I may have said something else, but I went to sleep before I heard what it was. Anyone who has gone to sleep driving a thruway knows the sensation—it is both agreeable and disagreeable. When I came awake I was still on my feet, but everything was in rapid sideways motion, with considerable overlap. Davidson and I were alone in the room. He was trying to get me to the couch, without actually picking me up and carrying me.

"What's this glub-glub stuff, Ben? Have you been hitting the vino?"

I put all my strength into forming one word he would understand. "Coffee."

"Coming right up, not that it's going to do you a hell of a lot of good."

I shook my head. For an instant I managed to open a path through the smog around me. I lunged at the coffee pot and knocked it off the table. Now if I went back to sleep before I got my message across, which seemed likely, Davidson wouldn't be tempted to sample the same loaded brew. Coffee splashed on my leg, but I didn't feel it.

"There goes your coffee," Davidson said.

I pushed against him feebly, trying to keep him from putting me on the couch. Once I was horizontal I knew I was through.

"Mickey," I said. "Fake it. You."

Even to me it didn't make sense, but at least Davidson distinguished the separate words. He peered at me. His eyes were the only fixed points in the general swirl, and they kept me from going under.

"I'm beginning to get you, Ben. They mickeyed the coffee? What do you mean, fake it? Stay inside? Pretend I've passed out?"

I started a nod. Before I could complete it I was asleep. He must have laid me on the couch, because that was where I was when I woke up, but I wasn't aware of being handled. I was too busy dreaming. The only thing I remember about those dreams is that they weren't pleasant.

Chapter 2

I heard somebody groaning. It was probably me. I opened my eyes. I was alive, and sorry about it. I had all the symptoms of the classic hangover with the one exception of remorse. I couldn't remember anything I had done to deserve this, and it didn't seem fair.

After a long moment I decided that the noise I was hearing was not, after all, a cat being tortured, but merely somebody whistling. I didn't want to think harshly of anyone, for my skull felt fragile enough to be shattered by that kind of thought, but in my opinion anyone who would make such a racket in a sick-room should be sprinkled with sugar and buried up to his neck in an anthill. Very slowly I turned my head.

A figure swam into view. It was nobody I wanted to see in my present condition. His name was Hamilton, and he had charge of security arrangements for a group of insurance companies that sold package policies covering homeowners against everything but acts of God. He was thin and dapper, with an ebbing hairline and a narrow, nervous mustache which seemed to have landed on his upper lip by accident. Whistling cheerfully between his teeth, in no known scale, he was checking the wedding presents against a list in a blue-bound folder.

I put my hand inside my jacket and checked to be sure the .38 was still in the rig. After that I looked at my watch. It was nearly 9:30. That was presumably 9:30 a.m. I had lost eleven hours.

I raised myself on one elbow. The change in altitude put me back on my revolving seesaw. That was as far as I was going for the time being. I could see nothing but a fine haze of whirling black dots. I tried to clear my throat; it came out as another groan.

"Nothing like a good night's sleep," Hamilton observed.

I liked him less and less, and I hadn't liked him at all to start with. "What are you doing out here?"

"Running inventory. Nothing much seems to be missing, which is lucky, Ben. But that's what I've noticed about you. You could fall in a garbage scow and come out in a Hart, Schaffner and Marx suit."

I put my feet on the floor and managed to sit up. For the first time since opening my eyes I considered the possibility that I might survive.

"Where's Davidson?"

"Around. Good man, Davidson. When you called yesterday and told me you needed a helper, you'll remember I wasn't too enthusiastic. I didn't want to authorize the expense. But you knew your limitations, Ben. I'll give you credit for that. You knew what would happen when they began passing out the free champagne."

"What are you talking about?"

"Now don't tell me you're going to insist on that coffee story. I see how you'd think it was a wonderful idea late at night, but look at it in the cold light of nine o'clock in the morning."

"Didn't Davidson tell you what happened?"

"Oh, Davidson's going to back you up. It doesn't surprise me."

I had both hands on my knees, pushing down hard to keep from pitching forward. I was still in a delicate balance with my environment. I wasn't thinking any less favorably of Hamilton than before, but more must have showed. He took a backward step and said shrilly, "Don't think you can threaten me, Gates. It's a little late for that. I don't like to gloat, because I've been known to take a drink or two on occasion myself, and I have a faint idea how you must be feeling right now. But I've got no use for a man in your profession who doesn't know when to stop."

My head was filled with a sudden ominous thudding. Hamilton gave a little squeak.

"I'd like to see you get rough with me," he said. "I'd just like to see you. You think you're in trouble now, I'll show you *real* trouble. Stay here. I'll be back. There's a man who wants to ask you some questions."

He went out, walking on the balls of his feet, and gave the door a slam which nearly took off the top of my skull, like someone opening a three-minute egg. Things had been coming at me a little too fast. It was now necessary to stand up and cross the room, which seemed as far as from Little America to the South Pole, over equally difficult terrain. Once there, I looked at myself in a mirror. It was a bad moment. I looked worse than I felt, which I wouldn't have said was possible. I looked as though I had fallen out of a boxcar which had been sealed for a transcontinental trip. The scratches had bled freely, and the girl had left quite a bit of lipstick on and around my mouth. Naturally I needed a shave, and my clothes looked as though they had been slept in, which was true. I straightened my tie and combed my hair with my fingers. Moistening my fingertips, I scrubbed at the lipstick, spreading it over a wider area. I needed soap and hot water. I needed a clean shirt. I needed three weeks in a rest home.

The door opened and Hamilton came back with Davidson and a man I hadn't seen before. He was well over six feet, and didn't have much fat on him except around the mouth. He had an abundant crop of iron-gray hair, and I diagnosed him at once as the kind of extremist who gets a weekly haircut. The fat lips smiled at me, showing teeth that were too beautiful to be his own.

"The Sleeping Beauty," he said. He made a big point of looking at the lipstick. "Awakened by a kiss."

Here was somebody else I could hate. "Who is this, Irving?"

Davidson had clearly been up all night. There were heavy shadows beneath his eyes.

"This is Lieutenant Minturn of the State cops," he said. "And you might as well know right now that he doesn't believe anybody served you a bad cup of coffee."

"I don't believe in Friday the thirteenth either," Minturn said heartily. "Haven't for years. But I can't blame you for trying."

He kicked against something. Stooping, he picked up a champagne bottle and set it on the table beside the girl's overturned glass.

I went back to work on the smeared lipstick. "There must be some coffee left in the pot. Have it analyzed."

"The pot has been removed," Davidson said, "by person or persons unknown. Also the cup and saucer. Here, for God's sake." He gave me a folded handkerchief. "Maybe I should have carried the goddam pot around with me all night, but I had other things on my mind. A doctor looked at you at one point, and he said to let you sleep it off."

I looked around and he said angrily, "Why should I take you to a hospital and pump you out? It was all over by then."

"What was all over?"

Minturn said quickly, "Now just a minute, Gates. I want to get your story first, if you don't mind."

Of course I minded, but he seemed to outrank me. I finished at the mirror, refolded Davidson's handkerchief with the smears inside and returned it to him. By keeping my mind on what I was doing, I got back to the couch without falling down. I lowered myself carefully.

"What would make you feel better, Ben?" Davidson asked. "Coffee?" Then he said hastily, "Excuse me. No coffee."

He lit a cigarette and gave it to me. After dragging on it once, I gave it back.

Minturn pulled a chair out from the wall and reversed it before sitting down, closer to me than I liked.

"Take it from the top, Gates. When did you start drinking?"

"I had my first beer when Repeal came in," I said. "I was nine at the time. But I know that's not what you mean. I didn't do any drinking last night at all."

"Now, Gates," he said, "we're grown-up people, so talk grown-up. If somebody went to the trouble of drugging your coffee, why wouldn't they make sure Davidson got some of the same?"

"He was out in the parking area," I said. "I called him in because I was having trouble with one of the bridesmaids. That was an accident. For another thing, he didn't get out here from New York till five-thirty or six. They may have thought I was working alone."

He shook his head. "Sorry. Now I'll tell you what *I* think happened. That glass over there has lipstick on it. I think a girl came in with a bottle and called you chicken until you had a drink with her. After that you had a few more drinks. Then you had sense enough to start to worry. You called New York and asked for Davidson. Hamilton says you already sounded a little high."

I cut my eyes at my ex-associate, who said hurriedly, "I didn't say that, Lieutenant. I said it was possible. There was so much noise in the background—"

Minturn went on, "And when you felt the room beginning to spin, you called Davidson in and told him what to say in case anything happened. He's no amateur. He knows enough to rinse out a coffee pot, if there *was* any coffee pot."

"Lieutenant—" Davidson said in a soft voice.

"Hold it, Irving," I said. "Maybe if we're patient we'll find out what he has in mind."

Minturn puffed his lips in and out, getting up a head of steam. Hamilton put in, "I'd better warn you, Lieutenant. Gates has quite a reputation for brawling with cops."

"But not this morning," I said wearily. "I have a headache. His dentures are safe."

"You'll have more than a headache before I'm done with you," Minturn said. "Private detectives are one species of louse I can't feel tolerant about. We don't get many out here, which is just as well. When I saw you lying there crocked to the gills, lipstick on your face, two people dead in the house—"

My head snapped forward. "What two people?"

"And merely because you hadn't ever learned the meaning of the word responsibility—"

"Now wait," Hamilton said. "I hold no brief for Ben, I think his conduct has been atrocious, but I don't consider him entirely accountable for what happened upstairs. To a certain extent that was separate."

"I can't agree with you," Minturn snapped. "If he'd been on the ball it wouldn't have happened. He's the precipitating factor. The guy came in, saw Gates lying on the sofa in a goddam drunken stupor, and thought he'd help himself. While he was about it, why not go upstairs first and try for two?"

I was drumming my fingers on my knee. "I think you mentioned a couple of deaths."

"Just a couple," Minturn said, giving me the same cold eye a teenage delinquent gets from Judge Leibowitz, "and it's God's mercy there weren't more. Quite a few shots were fired. I still haven't decided if I'm going to file formal charges of misconduct with the Secretary of State or not. I want to sleep on it first. It's not as bad as it might be. The jewelry's all been recovered—"

"Except for the one bracelet," Hamilton said. "And that we can take out of Ben's bond. I doubt if he'll ever get a surety company to write him another."

"My point exactly," Minturn said. "I promised myself I was going to have his license, but now I don't know if it's necessary. His publicity is going to be very bad, as he'll find out when he sees the afternoon papers. Not that I look on that version as final. By no means. If Gates and Moran worked out this stunt together—"

I broke in. "There's a name. And just who is Moran?"

"Leo Moran," Davidson said. "If the lieutenant will give me a minute?"

Minturn hesitated. "Go ahead, but make it brief. I want to see how he takes it, not that it matters a hell of a lot."

Davidson sat on one arm of the couch and flicked a nonexistent ash from his cigarette. "You had it figured, Ben," he said, without looking at me. "If I'd been standing up with a pistol butt sticking out of my coat, he would have turned around and gone home. But no. I'm just on the Jay-Vees around here. I did what you told me."

"None of this false modesty," Minturn said. "I don't

like it. You'll notice that when I was talking to the
newspaper boys I gave you full credit."

"Thanks," Davidson said. "It'll probably bring me in
loads of business. Now if you don't mind?"

"Go ahead, go ahead."

"I stretched out in a chair," Davidson said. "It was
a comfortable chair and I damn near went to sleep
myself before he came in."

"When was this?" I said.

"Just before midnight. Good-looking guy, gone to
seed a little. He took a quick look and went back to
the hall for one of those folding caterer's baskets. You
know what I mean. Aluminum framework covered
with purple canvas. I had a hard time keeping my eyes
shut, because it occurred to me that he might want to
sap us to make sure we were really out. But he went
straight to the jewelry table and began shoveling stuff
in. Am I boring you, Ben?"

"Not yet."

"I took out my gun. When that happens on television they put their hands up. But he grabbed out his
own gun and it went off. You'll find a hole in the back
of the couch right where you're sitting, Ben. It didn't
miss you by more than a whisker. You went on snoring."

He studied the end of the cigarette. "According to
the number of rounds I had left when it was over, I
fired five times. I hit him with three of them. He lost
quite a bit of blood going down the hall. I got him
again as he went over the railing of the terrace, and
that one did it. He had the container under his arm

and it broke when he landed. Diamonds were scattered around the lawn like dandelions."

"That's one," I said. "Who else is dead?"

"Mrs. Pope," Davidson said. "That necklace she was wearing must have been quite tempting to anybody who likes that kind of trinket. She kept it in a wall safe in her bedroom, and when she opened the safe to put it away, he jumped out at her. He was wearing one of those Halloween horror masks. The lady had a heart history, it seems. She fell down dead. He had some adhesive tape to tie her up, but he didn't need to use it. He got all the junk in the safe as well as what she was wearing. A very nice take."

"Fully covered by insurance," Hamilton observed.

"Is there any doubt about the cause of death?" I said.

"None whatever," Minturn said. "And if I remember rightly, this would qualify Moran for second-degree murder, even if he never laid a finger on her. But it's academic. You can't indict a corpse. So that about does it."

I disagreed, but before I could say anything there was a faint tapping at the door. A girl came in.

She was the new acquaintance I had made the night before. Everybody I had seen so far this morning had been the worse for wear, and she was no exception. She was wearing a white blouse and a flannel skirt, and she seemed to be built to different specifications now that she had shoes on. The specifications were still very nice, however. Her lipstick, which happened to be the same shade I myself was wearing, had been applied with care. There were lines on her face that hadn't been there when I saw her last—tiny pain wrinkles on her forehead and marks beneath her eyes.

And she had brought the diamond bracelet she had boosted from under my nose the night before, just before the roof fell in.

Chapter 3

"Excuse me," she said shakily. "I know I shouldn't be bothering you, but I thought—"

Hamilton swooped down on the bracelet. "That's the one, all right," he announced. "Forty-one hundred dollars. Now suppose you tell us where you got it."

"I'm not really sure." She looked about the room. When she saw me her lips made a small mechanical movement, not quite a smile. "Oh. Good morning. I'm a little vague about last night. I was pretty terrible, wasn't I?"

"You were pretty drunk," I said. "First you thought it would be fun to try on a bracelet and see what I'd do. I locked the door and called Davidson. Then your fiancé, or your ex-fiancé, banged on the door and you thought it would be fun to make him jealous. That's how the lipstick got on my face. That's all that happened, but you couldn't expect a cop to believe anything so obvious."

She looked at Davidson. "I didn't realize you were—"

"This is Lieutenant Minturn," I said.

"How do you do?" she said. "I'm Shelley Hardwick. At least I *think* I am. I'm going to stay away from weddings for a while. I'm sorry to say it probably happened just the way Mr.—?"

"Gates," I said.

"The way Mr. Gates says it did. It *sounds* like me, after champagne. When I woke up this morning I couldn't imagine where I got this bracelet, but I was pretty sure it was one of the wedding presents. I didn't think they gave bracelets away yesterday for favors. I was hoping to get it back before anyone knew it was missing."

Hamilton made a check mark in his folder. "That's the complete list, Lieutenant. I'm afraid he's in the clear."

The marks between the girl's eyes deepened. "Surely you didn't think Mr. Gates had—" Her eyes went from the empty champagne bottle to the glass and back to my face. "But that's absurd."

"It's absurd, all right," I said. "But private detectives are very uncouth. One drink of champagne and they go wild. You came in alone, and where you made your mistake was taking off your shoes. It's not every day I find myself alone in a room with a barefooted bridesmaid. I locked the door and tried to steal a kiss. You scratched my face, which was the least I deserved. At that point I switched tactics, and gave you a diamond bracelet. Luckily Davidson came in before I could get really ugly. That's the police theory, and if you'd ever tried to get a theory out of a cop's head you wouldn't try it this time."

"But it isn't true!" she cried, and added, "Is it?"

"That's immaterial," Lieutenant Minturn said. "Don't get yourself all worked up about poor persecuted Gates, Miss Hardwick. He goofed in a big way, but there's no charge against him. He's free to go."

She looked at me. "I've made it worse, haven't I?"

"It was bad enough already."

"But—I don't understand," she said. "I know I'm not functioning too well this morning, so maybe you'd better not explain it to me."

Hamilton put the bracelet back on the table. She gave it a final tender glance.

"Goodbye, you lovely thing."

She repeated the slight lip movement, which was probably intended as a smile, and went out.

"Pretty well stacked," Minturn observed. "Now that I've seen that, Gates, I'm not so surprised. It's Antony and Cleopatra all over again. Love conquers duty." He stood up. "You must have a lot to do somewhere. Don't let us keep you."

I would have preferred to do it standing up, but I was too feeble. "I won't try to change your mind. I like girls, but I don't give them other people's diamond bracelets. You can't be expected to know that. I can see why your version appeals to you. You hardly ever get a case which is solved by the time you get there. Moran killed Mrs. Pope, Davidson took care of Moran. Quick action by Lieutenant Minturn of the State Police led to the recovery of the stolen jewelry. Ben Gates is a drunken bum, but let's not worry about that. There's just one thing that bothers me. Did you ever hear of a job like this without an inside man?"

"What's your point, Gates?" Minturn said impatiently.

"Moran must have been hiding in Mrs. Pope's bedroom until she opened the safe."

"There's quite a big closet, almost a dressing room. He was probably in there. What about it?"

"He was taking quite a chance. How did he know there was enough in the safe to make it worth his while?"

"We're bearing that in mind. This investigation isn't finished, by any means."

"The simplest way to go about it," I said, "would be to find out who put that charge in my coffee."

He gave a little howl, as though I had jabbed him with something sharp. "I might have known. All right, for the sake of argument. Say somebody tipped him off about Mrs. Pope's habits, where she kept the jewelry and so on. Some disgruntled servant or ex-servant. Moran's dead. If this hypothetical accomplice took the precaution of having nothing to do with the actual robbery he or she has nothing to fear. The Pope family has suffered a terrible tragedy. I, for one, see no reason to make things worse by a lot of snooping and prying that can only muddy the waters."

"Yes, he's probably a big taxpayer," I said.

"That has nothing to do with it," Minturn snapped. "Hamilton, I take it that Gates is no longer employed by you?"

"That is correct," Hamilton said, taking little bites at the words. "And looking into my crystal ball, I'd say it's unlikely he will be employed by us in the future."

"That would seem to leave you without status, Gates," Minturn said. "But I don't want to seem unreasonable. If I come across anything that tends to bear out your story, I'll let you know."

"I'm sure you will," I said. "Would you mind if I have a word with the cook before, I go?"

"I would, as a matter of fact. Only one person is going to be asking questions in this house. That's me. Take my advice. Don't hang around the neighborhood. Go back to New York."

That was a piece of advice I didn't intend to take, and he probably knew it, for he said more emphatically, "You've got to ride with this one, Gates. It would be a lot of trouble for me to get a special hearing convened to suspend your license. A lot of trouble and a lot of paperwork, but if you force me to, I'll just have to go to that trouble."

We continued to look at each other. I was fascinated by the teeth. They would have made a wonderful prop for a hypnotist. He still didn't think he had made himself clear. He added, "This is my neck of the woods out here, Gates."

"Can I wash?" I said. "And I'd appreciate a couple of aspirin and a bicarb."

"Certainly," he said, relaxing.

I glanced at Davidson as I stood up. I didn't need to say anything; he got the message.

Minturn called one of his men. This one was wearing full regalia, including the musical-comedy hat. Minturn turned on his teeth in a final smile, all but blinding me. He gave my shoulder a dig with his bunched fingers.

"Next time better stick to Coca-Cola," he said. "If there is a next time."

Hamilton snickered. All this made it perfectly clear. They didn't have to disturb the Secretary of State, who was a busy politician. I could keep my license, but it might as well be void for any good it would do me. No private detective who gets drunk and falls asleep in the midst of the wedding presents he is being paid to guard can expect to go on getting business.

The trooper took me to a bathroom. He had the delicacy to wait outside. I washed carefully, but the scratches opened up again. By the time I had them under control I looked a good deal less sinister. I found an electric razor in the medicine cabinet, and I have to admit I used a toothbrush that didn't belong to me, a crime only a little less serious than insulting the flag. Then I lit a cigar and waited for the aspirin to take hold.

Finally the trooper knocked on the door. I gave it a few more minutes before going out. He was annoyed by the delay. Having gathered from Minturn that it wasn't necessary to be polite, he took me by the arm, as though feeling my muscle.

I stood still. I have a prejudice against being bounced, especially by cops.

"As a matter of procedure," I said, "there's been a death in the family, and the lieutenant doesn't want any unnecessary commotion. There will be one if you don't let go of my arm."

After a moment he let go. It was a small victory, but it didn't make me feel any better.

The undertaker's people couldn't have arrived in force, but the house had that strange hush that goes with the period before a funeral. I looked into the living room as I passed. Ten or twelve serious and well-dressed people were gathered there. The only one I recognized was Junior, standing in front of a raised fireplace holding a drink, like an ad for Scotch. He had been red in the face when I saw him last, but he was pale now, as though he had donated more blood to the Red Cross than he could spare. He was wearing a dark suit and a dark tie, and the highball was also very dark, the rich hand-rubbed color of undiluted whiskey. He caught my eye, and the drink halted halfway to his mouth.

I went past. One of the troopers at the door grinned and said something to a colleague. Outside, a photographer jumped down from a railing.

"Aren't you Ben Gates?" he said.

Now I knew how criminals feel when they pull their hats in front of their faces to keep from being photographed. Unfortunately I wasn't wearing a hat.

"That's right," I said pleasantly.

His camera came up. "They tell me you slept through the excitement. How's the hangover this morning, pretty painful?"

He tripped the shutter, hoping to catch a reaction his paper could use.

I smiled forgivingly. "I was off duty at the time, so I'd better let Lieutenant Minturn issue the statements. This is the first time we've worked together, but he impresses me as a highly competent police officer. It's obvious that Moran wasn't a loner. He had help from inside, and we're working on that now. I'm not at liberty to say anything more. What's the matter, Jack? You're not getting this down."

He closed his mouth and fumbled in his pocket for pencil and paper.

On the lawn, the caterer's men were striking the marquee. They hadn't begun the large task of policing up the empty bottles. The trooper took me all the way to my Buick, and watched me drive off. I checked the rear-view mirror at the foot of the drive; he was still watching. It was a big house, dating from a period when servants were more numerous and less costly. Davidson, I knew, was also watching from one of the many windows, to see which way I turned. I flashed the directional blinker, took the turn toward the parkway, and stopped at the first gas station. I told the attendant to fill the tank and see if the Buick needed anything else. I went into a lunchroom next to the station. I had to order something, so I ordered coffee. When it came I did my best to ignore it.

A car pulled up outside and Davidson came in. He took the stool next to mine.

"What do they put in the coffee here, Ben?"

"Just coffee, I hope."

He laid a slip of paper on the counter. "That's the maid's name. The address is in Prosper, a couple of miles down the road. She was hired for the night. They call her when they need somebody special for a dinner or a party."

I put the paper in my pocket. He ordered coffee and a repulsive kind of pastry, and when the waitress had returned to her post at the cash register he said, "In confidence, Ben—how much did you drink last night?"

I was still convalescing. I started violently, nearly knocking over a ketchup bottle. "Please, Irving."

"Well, you were coming out with some of the damnedest snores. You certainly *sounded* drunk. But it was the coffee?"

"It was the coffee," I said.

"All right. I suppose I believe you. I talked to the cook. She's a little hungover herself this morning, and she wasn't too helpful. She had a gallon pot of coffee on the stove all evening, and when anybody wanted some they helped themselves. She thinks Pope's secretary, somebody named Miss DeLong, suggested that the man in the library might be hungry."

"Who filled the small pot? The cook or the girl who brought it up?"

"The cook. Her name's Mrs. Maguire. And there was something about sandwiches. People were coming and going all the time. The girl could have set the tray down when she went out to the buffet. Mrs. Maguire doesn't know how the empty pot got back to the kitchen, or who washed it and put it away. In other words, the dice are chilly, Ben. She didn't want to talk to me much, and those troopers were breathing down the back of my neck. I paid five bucks for this small amount of information. You'll get a bill."

"Are you working on anything right now?"

He sighed. "I was afraid that was coming. Would I get paid?"

"Have you ever done any work for me and not been paid?"

"No-o-o," he said. "But this is a little unusual, wouldn't you say? I don't mean I won't do it. I just want to keep it under the counter. Minturn is the big law-enforcement man around here, and he's already hinted that he can throw me some business, lucky me."

"What do you make of him, Irving?"

"He seems to be a pretty good cop. But I gather that Pope Senior has strong political connections, based on his generosity when they come around begging for money. It may be that Minturn has had the word. I'd say he's being more of the feudal serf than the situation calls for."

"Are you due back?"

"Yeah, they're probably looking for me now. I'm their number-one gunslinger, after all."

His hand shook as he lifted his mug; some of the coffee slopped over. "Well, hell, Ben," he said after taking a noisy sip and putting the mug on the counter, "that was a long, noisy night. I never shot at anything but a paper target before."

"There's a first time for everything," I said without sympathy. "How did they make the identification on Moran?"

"Fingerprints. He came in a stolen car with a city number, so they checked his prints with New York. His record came in just before you woke up. Two arrests, one for conspiracy to defraud, the second for sending pornographic matter through the mails. No convictions. And to me this looks a little weird. A New

York angle-man wouldn't go robbing in the country unless he thought it was open and shut."

I thought for a moment. "How about Mrs. Pope? Who found her?"

"Mr. Pope. He sleeps in the next room, with a bathroom between. When he heard the shots downstairs, he ran into her room. Something came in on that while you were taking your time shaving. They've got the official cause of death. Coronary occlusion. Does that sound right? Heart attack, as everybody figured."

"Did you hear anything about my playmate, this Shelley Hardwick?"

"Three of the bridesmaids spent the night, and she was one of them. She thinks she heard shots. The cops did a lot of tramping through the house later, and you know how they are about using sirens, but she was like you. She didn't wake up."

"Where does she stand with Junior? That's a thing of the past?"

"It didn't come up. All I know is what I heard last night, and you may remember that I walked into that without being briefed. She said something about keeping the ring, though—I didn't get much of it."

"Maybe I dreamed this, but didn't he threaten to kill her?"

Davidson turned to me. "Sure he did. And she said, 'You've had practice,' or something like that."

"And what did she say about White Plains?"

He worked at it for a minute. "She followed him there. Or did he follow her? No, she followed him. Wait a minute, Ben, wait a minute. Who do you think lives in White Plains? Mr. Pope's secretary. This Anna DeLong."

"I thought she was in residence."

"No, I was there when Minturn took her statement. She slept over last night because of the wedding."

I had forgotten I had a headache. Davidson, too, was looking almost cheerful. I lifted my coffee, remembered suddenly how I was feeling, and put it down.

"I'll check on the maid," I said. "I've been wondering how she would look out of uniform. Keep close to Minturn. The main thing I want now is anything that comes in on Moran."

Chapter 4

The name on the slip of paper was Hilda Faltermeier. I drove on to the little town of Prosper. Instead of wasting time and attracting attention by asking for directions, I left the Buick in an A & P parking lot and crossed to the taxi stand at the New York Central station. I got into the first of two cabs and gave the driver the address that went with the name.

We left the shopping area and passed through a zoned neighborhood that had probably produced most of the cars parked at the station waiting for the head of the house to come back from New York on the evening trains. Soon after this we entered one of those sad developments that were thrown up in the hell-for-leather days after World War II. Hurricanes are infrequent in this part of the country, so the houses were still standing, but it worried me to see a boy bouncing a rubber ball against a wall.

The driver stopped in the middle of a block. I told him to wait. I went up a short walk and knocked on a screen door.

"Come on in," a girl's voice called. "It's not locked."

I went in. Hilda Faltermeier was up on a stepladder painting a wall yellow.

"Why, Mr. Gates," she said. "This is an honor."

She was wearing a tight pair of jeans spattered with

yellow paint, and a shirt with most of the buttons missing. Instead of being tucked inside the pants, her shirt-tails were knotted in front, leaving an uncovered strip of flesh near the equator. She was barefoot, and I hoped I wouldn't have the same trouble with her that I'd had with the barefoot Shelley Hardwick.

She came down the ladder. Her hair was two shades of light brown, but she had darkened her eyebrows and lashes. She was in her early twenties, and if she wasn't married already I didn't think she would stay unmarried long.

"Painting," she said unnecessarily. "How's the private detective business?"

"About the same. How did you know my name was Gates?"

"The girls were talking about you last night. Most of us hadn't ever seen a real live private detective, and we thought you were pretty stimulating. You know how girls are?"

"Within limits." I took out a cigar and began peeling off the cellophane. "What I wanted to ask you—"

"Come on in and sit down," she said. "I don't suppose you'd be drinking this early in the day, but how about some—"

"No coffee, thanks," I said.

"Sit down anyway."

I followed her through an open arch and sat on a couch facing the blank eye of a television set. The room was pleasantly furnished, and somebody had put in a lot of work with vacuum cleaner and furniture polish.

"My Dad's at work," she said, "if that's what you're thinking. So we have the place to ourselves."

"That's not what I was thinking."

She settled on a sort of hassock, tucking one foot under her. She had fewer buttons on her shirt than I had thought at first. Even with close scrutiny, and this is a matter which I like to give close scrutiny, I could only count one.

"Anyway, it's flattering," she said, "because I look like Whistler's mother in that damn lace cap I have to wear at the Popes'. Anybody who could see I'm worth following up in spite of that cap must have X-ray vision."

I bit the end off the cigar. "Do you always put on eye makeup this early, even when you're not expecting anybody?"

She gave a little laugh. "All right, I knew you were coming. Mrs. Maguire called me."

"What did she say?"

"Oh—somebody brainwashed her for my name and address, and they figured he probably passed it on to you. They want me to watch out, because you're supposed to be pretty shifty. Can I ask a question? How old are you?"

"Thirty-four."

"That's what I thought, but we had an argument about it last night. How about the other detective? The one outside? He's not nearly as old as that, is he?"

"Not nearly," I said. "His name is Davidson, if you ever need anybody in our business. Miss Faltermeier—"

"I don't expect to need a private detective," she

said, "I mean professionally. Not that I have anything
against private detectives."

"I'm glad to hear that. What I'm trying to—"

"And if I ever get in that kind of trouble, which I
certainly hope I won't, I think I'd call you, Mr. Gates,
if I had to choose."

"Thanks a lot. Now I'd like to find out if anybody
said anything to you last night about taking coffee out
to Davidson."

She crossed her legs in a modified yoga position.
The blue jeans had been tight enough when she was
standing up, and they were tighter now.

"That's a funny question."

"It's one I'd like an answer to, though," I said. "When
Mrs. Maguire told you to take coffee to the library, did
she say anything about taking another pot out to the
man on the terrace?"

"No, she didn't. I didn't even know he was a private
detective then. He looked like one of the guests, only
not so drunk!"

"After Mrs. Maguire poured the coffee, do you
remember what you did with it? Did you set it down
any place?"

"No, I came straight upstairs. I got the sandwiches
first. Those little silver coffee pots don't hold the heat."

"Did you talk to anybody?"

"Well, you know what it was like. I had an admirer,
one of the ushers. He'd been following me around for
a couple of hours, and we had a little scuffle on the
stairs. If Miss DeLong hadn't been right behind us
I would have had to go back to heat up the coffee.

He was quite cute, really, but *so* tight. The next time they ask me to serve out there I'm going to wear a girdle."

"Were you still around when the guns went off?"

"I should say. I got through at eleven-thirty, and then I had to change. They have these little closets up in the attic where the servants used to live; no heat in cold weather and brutal in summer. And of course this same boy was waiting on the stairs for me when I came down. We played Run, Sheep, Run up the front stairs and down the back. It was like one of those old-time movies. Are you interested?"

"Sure. What happened?"

"He didn't catch me, so you can take the leer off your face. But he wore me out. One time he had me cornered and I didn't think I was going to make it. Luckily somebody came out of a bedroom—"

"Who?"

"I don't know what her name was. A blonde. I think she was one of the bridesmaids, but this was after her bedtime and she had on a kimono, very Japanesey. The way my boyfriend's mind was working, a girl is a girl, and this girl was already partly undressed, which would save time. But she was too quick for him, so back to the class struggle. I got outside all right. I headed for the front of the house. You probably don't remember hinting that you might be waiting for me, but I thought if you happened to be there I'd let you rescue me. I didn't get that far. You can't run very fast on a lawn in high heels. Don't think I wasn't trying to get away, because I was. He tackled me. Did you ever read *Anatomy of a Murder?*"

"I saw the movie."

"Well, it didn't go quite that far because that's when the shooting started. My boy kept on trying until a body came over the railing and nearly landed on us. That was the end, as far as romance was concerned. Now you see what you missed by falling asleep."

"To go back to the coffee. You didn't take the empty pot down to the kitchen?"

"I didn't even think of it. What's all this about coffee?"

"If you'll put your feet on the floor for a minute, I'll tell you."

She got out of her yoga position with a smile. "I didn't know it was bothering you."

"I'm not that middle-aged. I don't know what you heard about last night, but I didn't have anything to drink except one cup of coffee out of that pot you brought me. Five minutes later I was out cold. How does it look to you?"

She got up for a cigarette. The cigarettes were on a low table in front of the couch. She had to bend over, and the shirt responded to the pull of gravity. The hell she didn't know she was bothering me.

She lighted the cigarette, pretending to think about my problem. "Gee—I don't know. I had the sandwiches. I poured the coffee. I didn't meet anybody on the stairs but Miss DeLong."

Instead of going back to the hassock, she dropped

onto the couch beside me, sitting side-saddle with one leg up. "And she didn't come anywhere near the tray. As for Prince Charming, he had me doing a ballet dance, but I don't think he fooled with the coffee pot. He didn't have any hands free, for one thing. Just thinking about it gives me goose pimples."

She gave a little wriggle.

"How often do you work at the Popes'?"

"Oh, depending. Sometimes once or twice a week, sometimes not again for a month. Why?"

"I was wondering about Richardson, Junior. Did he ever tell you you have a very cute navel?"

She looked down at her bare midriff and laughed. "In the uniforms I wear out there it doesn't show. If you mean did he ever tackle me from behind and try to lay me in the bushes, the answer is no."

"Well—"

I made a small forward movement and she said quickly, "Don't go."

I drew carefully on my cigar. I like cordial girls, but perhaps this one was being too cordial.

"Why not?"

She came up on both knees, letting the shirt take care of itself. The final button was hanging by a thread. "If you really didn't do any drinking last night, what about that conversation you had with me when I brought up your tray?"

"What about it? All I'd been doing since noon was standing around drawing three dollars an hour plus expenses, in this case nil. You broke the monotony."

"Mmm," she said thoughtfully. "I didn't pay too much attention because I thought you'd been sampling the champagne. This makes a difference."

"I don't see why."

"You don't?"

She wriggled again, walking on her knees. She touched the back of my neck. This is a sensitive spot for me, as girls seem to know. The next instant she was all over me. It didn't seem likely that the single button could stand the strain.

"I've got a taxi waiting," I said. "It's costing me money."

"There are more important things in life than money."

That was perfectly true. The poor child was lonely, with nothing to do all day but paint walls and look at TV. I could spare a few minutes.

She shifted position, and the crucial button came off with a pop.

"Just as I suspected," I said. "You're a girl."

She was smiling. "Don't you like girls?"

"In their place. Can I call you Hilda?"

"I wish you would."

"Hilda, wouldn't you feel more comfortable if I took off my gun?"

She drew back. She looked at me for a moment and then shrugged. In the open shirt it was an attractive gesture.

"All right, on your way."

"In other words, this was a stall?"

"You can call it that," she said. "Now if I were you, Ben, which thank God I'm not, I'd blow."

"In a minute," I said. "Who really called you, Minturn?"

"I didn't get his name. Some lieutenant. He said if I wanted to go on working at the Popes' I should keep you entertained till he could get a radio car over from the barracks. They want to talk to you."

"What about?"

"Ben, will you kindly spring into action? I don't want to change my mind and then have them catch you anyway. He said they're working on a theory that you were in for a percentage last night. You knocked yourself out with sleeping pills so you'd be covered, and now you're squawking because somebody washed the coffee pot and you can't prove it."

"That's even worse than their first theory." I stood up. "But I don't think they really want to discuss it with me. They just want to give me the rush."

"You can move faster than that."

"You'd better sew some buttons on by the time they get here. You're breaking the law."

"Ben, hurry! How do you think I'll *feel*? I should have told you right away."

I stopped with my hand on the screen door and we looked at each other. They weren't using the siren, but they were coming fast.

"Damn you!" she said. "Goddam you, anyway!"

"What's all the excitement? They're only cops."

Tires screamed as they came around the corner.

They didn't have to look for street numbers; the taxi outside would show them the house they wanted. Suddenly the whole thing seemed unnecessarily urgent. It shouldn't have been this important for Minturn to keep me from talking to Hilda.

"Take my bike," she said.

"Your what?"

"My bike. It's in the garage. You can go out through the back yard."

"My dear girl," I said. "A bike. Don't you think they could catch me in a prowl car?"

She took my arm and urged me toward the kitchen. "I'll pass out. Come on, Ben. They'll have to bring me to before I can tell them what happened. I only wish I had more clothes on."

The police car came to a noisy halt in front of the house and two uniformed troopers jumped out. One of them was pulling at the flap of his pistol holster, and that decided me.

"I'll call you," I said. "Not that this is going to work."

I gave her a passing pat on the most inviting target and eased quietly out the back door as I heard the troopers' footsteps on the porch.

Chapter 5

The troopers gave me no trouble. I can't say the same for the bike.

I wheeled it across the yard, keeping the garage between me and the house. The boundary between this lot and the next was marked by a flower bed and a low wire fence. I stepped on some delphiniums, but I couldn't take the time to be careful. I was out in the open now, and I wanted to disappear before one of the troopers looked out Hilda's kitchen window.

When I was halfway to the street a woman came out with a basket of wet laundry.

"Good morning," I said cheerfully around my cigar. "Short cut."

She watched me, her mouth open. When I reached her driveway I swung aboard and pedaled off, biting down hard on my cigar. I hadn't been on one of these things for twenty years, and this one had a strong tendency to wobble. I straightened it out finally, and I thought I was going to be all right until I put on the brake at the first intersection. It was like stepping on a top step that wasn't there. The bike reared and bucked me into a barberry hedge.

I untangled myself, cursing the girl for offering me a bicycle without brakes. I discovered where the brakes actually were by squeezing the handlebars too hard and pitching forward over the front wheel. Before I started again I looked the contraption over for other concealed traps. I found a little lever that was probably a gear-shift, and decided to disregard it. Several housewives had come out on their porches to watch the entertainment. I got on again and managed to disappoint them by staying on. They may have wondered why a man of my years, wearing a business suit and smoking a cigar, should be riding a girl's bike down their street in the middle of the morning, but if so they didn't wonder about it enough to report it to anybody.

I took a roundabout route back to the shopping district. It was downhill most of the way. I was getting plenty of attention, but the bike made no further attempts to throw me. I left it with the ticket agent at the railroad station.

I passed up several outside phone booths and found one of the old-fashioned kind hidden in a drugstore. I dialed the Popes' number. Unless a cop answered, I still should be able to get Davidson on the phone.

A man's voice said hello.

"I'd like to talk to Irving Davidson," I said. "The insurance company detective."

"Who is this?"

"Mr. Shields, from the New York office."

There was a pause. I heard somebody breathing. The same voice said, "You wouldn't be kidding me, would you? Is your real name Gates?"

"That's right," I said. "I take it this is Junior?"

"I don't like even my friends to call me that," he

said, "so don't you. You're a persistent son of a bitch, aren't you?"

"Why do you say that? I haven't got around to you yet."

Pope let a moment go by and said, "Why should you want to get around to me?"

"I have one or two questions."

"I'm thrilled. But maybe you'd better make it some other day. I'm busy, and you might have trouble getting in. I don't know what you've done to Minturn. He had a phone call a few minutes ago, and he did a little yelling. I was in the next room with the door open, and if you make the mistake of showing up here, you are to be pounded on like a drum. We have quite a good fence around the property. Minturn told the sergeant to put a man at the foot of the drive to keep out the curiosity seekers. I believe that includes you."

"Thanks for the warning," I said. "I'm always interested in the reasons people have for not wanting to answer questions. What are yours?"

He made a disgusted sound and slammed down the phone.

I thought for a moment, then looked through the yellow pages of the county phone book. I dialed a number.

A hushed voice answered, "Morrison Mortuary. Mr. Morrison speaking."

"Sergeant Shea of the State Police," I said. "I'm making arrangements for traffic control at the Pope funeral. You'll be handling that, won't you?"

"Why, no," the voice said, surprised. "I understand

that Henry Turner—or so I was informed. Where did you hear—because we have every facility, and we'd be more than happy—"

"Turner," I said abruptly. "True enough. I should have written it down. Sorry to bother you."

I hung up, went back to the yellow pages and found the address of Henry J. Turner, Inc., Funeral Directors. I bought some cigars at the cashier's counter and asked for directions. A few minutes later I was outside Henry J. Turner's subdued show window, which displayed lilac drapes and a single large urn, presumably empty.

A bell tinkled as I went into a waiting room. Canned mood music was coming from somewhere. I didn't need it; I was feeling melancholy already. A young man came through from a back room, slipping on a dark coat. His hands were very clean and slightly wrinkled; he'd probably just been embalming somebody.

"Mr. Turner?" I said.

"No, Mr. Turner is out," he said with regret, as though he had just learned of the passing of one of my dear ones. "I am his co-worker, Leon Satterthwaite, if I can be of any assistance."

"Miss DeLong asked me to stop in," I said. "She's been trying to call you all morning. All she gets is a busy signal."

His hands clasped each other. He looked at me out of the tops of his eyes, like a springer spaniel who wants to go out.

"Miss DeLong. Mr. Pope's secretary. A terrible thing, wasn't it? We were all of us deeply shocked.

Such a vibrant woman, Mrs. Pope, so thoroughly alive."

"Miss DeLong was hoping Mr. Turner could come out."

Mr. Satterthwaite opened his eyes wide and unleashed his hands. "But he's there! He left two hours ago!"

"He never got there."

"What on earth? He did have one other bereaved party en route, but that was only scheduled to take a minute. Do you suppose he's been trying to get me? I'd better check my phone."

"Could you do that later?" I said. "Miss DeLong is getting impatient. I heard her say something about giving the contract to Morrison's, if you're too busy to handle it."

"But we aren't busy at all!" he exclaimed. "And even if we were up to capacity, which we aren't by any means, we would always make room for Mrs. Richardson Pope! You may remember the ceremony we handled for the Popes a few months ago. That unfortunate man, not much left of him to bury. Properly speaking we should have refused it, we were overloaded, but we burned the midnight oil, so to speak. I don't make a practice of running down competitors, heaven forbid. But Morrison simply hasn't the *stature*—I suppose he quoted you a lower price. There's more than price to a dignified interment, much, much more. I think I'll just run out myself and straighten this out."

He told someone in the rear to report the phone out of order, and came back putting his head into a black Homburg.

"Do you mind if I ride with you?" I said. "My car's in the garage."

"Not at all. Delighted."

He led me to a jet-black Cadillac, one of the seven-passenger sedans that are manufactured for undertakers and city officials. As he drove he described the elegant work his firm had done. Everything about a Henry J. Turner ceremony, in his possibly biased opinion, was in impeccable taste.

The police car at the entrance to the Popes' driveway was parked at a right angle, blocking one lane. The red light on the roof blinked compulsively. Satterthwaite slowed but didn't stop. I wished I had the added protection of a Homburg, but one in the front seat of a black Cadillac was enough; the troopers only gave me a glance.

"Hello!" Satterthwaite said, seeing another outsized Cadillac beside the house. "Henry made it, after all. That's a weight off my mind. While I'm here, I think I'll look in and see if I can make myself useful."

He steered the big car into an open space, removed his Homburg to run a pocket comb through his hair, and put the Homburg back on. I went in with him.

"This way," I said, guessing.

We had entered by a side door. I headed down the cross hall for the main entrance, hoping to find Davidson before anyone spotted me. After that I wanted to have a talk with Miss DeLong. There were two people I particularly didn't want to see. One was Lieutenant Minturn. The other was Richardson Pope, Jr., who at that moment came through an open door directly in our path. He was carrying four bottles of whiskey wrapped in tissue paper, two in each hand. Another boy his same age, with another four bottles, was behind him. Seeing me, Pope stopped so short that the other boy walked into him with a clash of glass.

"Hey, watch that good Johnny Walker," he said.

Pope had recovered some of his color, but it had come back in patches, giving him a mottled look. "Gates, my friend, you are an idiot. After all the advice I gave you, too. See what we have here, Binge."

His friend looked me over. He was built like a stump, without a waistline. His blond hair was cropped so close that his scalp shone through.

"This would be Gates, the bloodshot private eye?"

"That's who it would be. And it seems to me I told him nobody wanted to see him. Here," he said to Satterthwaite, loading him with bottles. "Take these to the thirsty people in the living room."

"Glad to," Satterthwaite said.

"Just follow the tinkle of ice cubes. Binge, show our friend one of your holds. I'll get Sonny."

He walked off quickly. Satterthwaite followed with the bottles. Binge stepped in against me and clamped both hands around my right arm, pressing his thumbs against the axillary nerve in the armpit. It is one of the basic judo come-alongs. It can be broken in a number of ways, one of which is to twist suddenly and kick your man in the stomach. Considering the recent bereavement the family had suffered, that didn't seem quite the thing to do here.

"That's all right," I said, rising on my toes to ease the pressure. "Where did you pick it up?"

"I wasted my youth in the Marines," Binge said, smiling happily. He stepped up the pressure, to see me rise another half inch.

Pope came back, accompanied by a tall, black-haired youth, considerably underweight, weaving like a sunflower in a wind.

"Talking about your military service?" Pope said. "Dishonorably discharged," he told me admiringly. "Plenty of people buck for it, but Binge is the man who got it."

"And it wasn't easy," Binge said.

"I'm going to have a little conference with Gates," Pope said. "Not in the house. We don't want to spoil the atmosphere. Let's show the man our swimming pool."

"Absolutely," Sonny agreed. "Where the cannibals cooked the missionary. He'd better watch his P's and Q's or he'll get some of the same."

"Sonny," Pope said sharply. "I've told you before. No cracks."

"Absolutely, no cracks."

They walked me out of the house. There was no doubt what they had in mind, and like so much else that had happened this morning, it seemed out of proportion. We went across the parking area, in a loose but definite formation. Minturn and a uniformed trooper came around the house. We were far enough apart so we didn't need to greet each other if we didn't want to, and neither of us wanted to. Minturn scraped his hand across his chin. I was back on Pope property against his wishes, but he decided to let Pope and his friends administer the discipline.

Skirting the garages, we went through a latticed arbor and came to a kidney-shaped swimming pool. The striped umbrellas and the usual swimming pool furniture were out, but naturally no one was in the pool. There was a low bathhouse. Beyond a putting green and a croquet lawn, I saw a blackened area where a building had recently burned down. Part of a brick chimney was all that remained.

"You had a fire?" I said.

"One of the dandiest fires you ever saw," Sonny said behind me.

Pope looked around and there was nothing further out of Sonny.

"I want privacy," Pope said. "The bathhouse."

"The men's side or the women's?" Binge asked, and Pope said, "Shut up, creep."

I thought we had enough privacy where we were. I whirled my right arm. Binge held on. Both his arms flew up, leaving his midsection open. I hit him with a left, a little low but not low enough to make him mad, and he let go. I completed the pivot and backed up against the bathhouse wall.

It was Sonny who surprised me. He spread out his long arms and toppled forward. I hit him sharply twice, but it was like trying to divert a falling spruce. His arms wrapped themselves around me; there seemed to be more than two. Before I could get untangled, Binge slid between me and the wall and clamped on one of the nastiest holds in the repertoire, pulling my arm behind my back and up toward the opposite shoulder. Now with only a little more lift, he could break the arm. He was too slow to be really good at this kind of argument, but to get away from him I would need more room. I couldn't do anything while I was hampered by Sonny.

"What do you want me to do, say uncle?"

"Inside," Pope said.

I pushed at Sonny with my left hand, and his arm slipped off my shoulder. That was apparently all that had been holding him up. He slid to the concrete.

Pope turned him over. He was peacefully asleep.

"He must have a glass jaw," Pope said scornfully. "How about it, Binge, can you manage the tough man from the big city?"

Binge sneered. "With my toes."

He steered me through the open door. I was glad to see that the floor inside was covered with duckboards. There were four cubicles to a side, each with a swinging door, several shower heads in a wider area beyond.

Pope stopped. "You haven't been smart, Gates. God knows I'm in no position to preach, but there's one thing I've learned—do something as dumb as you did last night, and you've got to take the consequences."

He showed me what he meant by consequences by throwing a right at my head. He wasn't aiming at anything important. Where it hurt most was in my arm socket as I went backward.

"I want to ask a question," I said.

His eyes narrowed. "You say that so politely, go ahead."

"Ease off on the pull, will you?" I said to Binge. "I don't mean let go. Just ease off a little."

He lowered my arm enough so my heels could touch the duckboards. "I've heard two theories about last night," I said. "Naturally I have one of my own. I'd like to know what really happened, but I don't want to learn any family secrets. It makes no difference to me how you spend your nights, or with how many people. Is that clear? All I want to know is who was working with Moran. Why should that bother you?"

"Nobody was working with Moran. He was working alone. That's one thing the police are sure of."

"They're sure because it's easier that way. Easier for them, easier for you and your father. They couldn't get a conviction, they probably couldn't even make an arrest, so why waste time thinking about it? Nobody's interested except me, but I'm very interested. Listen for a minute. You brought in extra servants for the night. The caterer must have had a dozen people. It almost has to be somebody from the outside who didn't know Davidson was here. So why is everybody getting so hysterical?"

Pope hadn't been listening. "That's crap and you know it. There's no such person. Nobody had to tell Moran there was a wedding here yesterday—it was in the papers. Mother was wearing her big necklace. He saw it and decided to make a stab at that too. Hell, it's so easy anybody can see it. He had a gun, didn't he? If he'd known you were going to be asleep, why would he bring a gun? He was planning to stick you up."

"People like that do carry guns," I said. "They feel more confident."

"Crap," Pope repeated. "Sheer crap. I heard Minturn explain it. You're in a jam. If you make enough noise, maybe you can get somebody to believe you. I talked to what's his name, Hamilton. He says you're going to be hurting for clients from now on, and I can't say my ass bleeds for you, either. Get a good hold, Binge. I'm going to work on his body first."

I had one more point to make, and I made it fast. "I said I wasn't after your secrets. But that's something that can change."

"This is going to be a sample, man," Pope said, showing me his right fist, not a terribly lethal weapon. "I'll say it now while you're conscious. You've been told to keep off our land. That didn't work, and maybe this will. But if you ever come back and annoy us again, you'll wish you hadn't."

He took his time, making a face as he drew back his fist. Binge raised my arm. But he had left me too much slack; I unbent my knees and went up and to the right, as if I had been doing a half-twist off a low board. There wasn't much spring in the duckboards, but Binge gave me the lift I needed, so I was past the danger point before I started to come down. I landed on one shoulder, and as my legs whipped around he lost his hold.

He chopped at me with the slicing edge of his palm. I took it on my forearm. I already had a foot behind his ankle, and I slammed the other against his kneecap. He went over, falling through one of the swinging doors.

Pope stamped at me. I rolled out from underfoot and I was halfway up when Sonny, conscious again, wavered in from the doorway and fell on me.

It was like being hugged by a languid octopus. Pope was shouting, jabbing at me with both fists at the same time, without taking the time to get set. He was hitting Sonny nearly as often as he was hitting me. Whenever I threw off one of Sonny's arms and went to work on the other, the first came back and wrapped itself around me. I was carrying the whole weight, and I didn't want to fall where Binge could get at me.

I heard a rush of footsteps. A girl's voice called, "Dick! Dick! What in God's name are you *doing?*"

Pope was having a small fit, Sonny and I were embracing, Binge was trying to stand up. That was the complete answer to the question. I caught a glimpse of a white blouse and a white face above it— Shelley Hardwick, and I didn't think she was going to be much help.

She cried, "Dick, don't you have any sense at all? Don't you know what—"

"Keep away from me," he yelled.

The interruption made him realize that he wasn't hurting me. Reaching past Sonny, he grabbed my neck in both hands. His lips were contorted and his eyes seemed to be in danger of starting out of his head. He had forgotten that all he wanted to do was warn me against trespassing. Now he wanted to kill me.

I almost went down. Suddenly Sonny gave a small grunt. He let go and started another downward slide. I brought my fists up hard between Pope's arms and knocked his fingers away from my throat. He came at me again. I sidestepped and hit him as he went by. He plunged into the shower, traveling the last few feet on his nose, and ended up against the wall. I went after him, feeling very mean. He looked up, but what he saw discouraged him. He stayed where he was.

I whirled. For the time being all was peaceful in the bathhouse. Binge had stopped trying to get up. He lay back against the door of one of the cubicles, whimpering and protecting his injured knee with both hands. Shelley was standing above Sonny, who was again unconscious. She was holding one of her high-heeled shoes by the toe. There was a small metal plate on the heel, and I assumed that this had recently made contact with Sonny's skull. Because of the spring in the arch, a high-heeled shoe is one of the most efficient saps ever devised.

"You realize you're on the men's side?" I said.

Her breath came out in a half-laugh. She balanced on one foot to put on her shoe.

I ran hot water into one of the basins. Pope started to move. I said wearily, "No, Dick," and he stopped.

I still wasn't sure it was over, and I watched him in the mirror for a moment.

"Now what?" he said.

"Now I think I'd better see your father," I said. "I didn't want to bother him today, but it looks as though he'll have to be bothered."

Pope made a funny sideways gesture. "I suppose you'll tell him."

I didn't answer. There was something slightly appealing about the boy, but I couldn't be expected to feel kindly toward someone who had just been trying to throttle me. I looked at the damage. It wasn't bad, although I had hardly looked my best to start with. Luckily Dick hadn't been wearing rings. The marks on my neck were beginning to fade.

I washed my hands and face and borrowed his comb. He stood behind me while I combed my hair.

"I guess I know how you feel," he said, "but I wish you wouldn't mention it to him, Gates. It would upset him. Don't you realize why I did it? I didn't want him to be disturbed."

"That's possible," I said. "But I don't know if it's true. I don't know why you and Shelley were yelling at each other last night. I don't know who told Moran there was jewelry in your mother's safe. I don't know why Shelley walked into this fight. Those are a few of the things I don't know."

Shelley protested, "I couldn't stand here and let them murder you, could I?"

I stooped to look at Sonny's head. Binge's jaws were clenched, but he couldn't keep little injured noises from escaping between his teeth.

"You'll need something to take your mind off what I'm saying to your father," I said to Pope. "The Marine needs a doctor. Leave him right here—don't try to move him. And have the doctor look at Sonny."

"Hell, you can't hurt Sonny," Pope said uneasily. His voice changed as he looked at Shelley. "And as for *you*, baby—"

"Dick," Shelley said, "I know it's expecting a lot, but *think*, will you?"

She came outside, still angry with me. "What do you mean, you don't know why I hit Sonny? What's so hard to understand about it? You don't know Dick Pope. He wasn't getting ready to let go."

"I was just feeling sorry for myself," I said. "Do you still want to hire a detective?"

"Oh, God. I suppose I said something last night."

"If you need a detective, I need a client. I've got to do something to get some official standing, not that it'll make much difference to Minturn."

"I haven't any money to hire a detective. It was just a crazy idea."

"Never mind about the money. Wait for me and we'll talk about it. Maybe I can give you a lift somewhere."

Chapter 6

Anna DeLong was an orderly looking girl in her middle twenties. She wore glasses, and when I had met her the day before, having that kind of a mind, I had wondered how much persuasion would be necessary to get her to take them off. Her black hair was pulled back severely and gathered in a small bun. That was something else that could be remedied by pulling a few pins. She had unusually clear skin and a calm manner, giving the impression of always knowing exactly where to put her hand on a well-sharpened pencil. If her checkbook ever failed to balance, it would be the fault of the bank. Sometimes, I know, this manner in a secretary is a danger signal. Suddenly, for no apparent reason, she will break the points of her pencils and have to be restrained from walking in and telling her boss what she thinks of him. In Miss DeLong's case, I thought the calmness was genuine.

She had worn a black suit the day before, to make it clear that she was on the payroll and not a guest, and she was wearing the same suit today, with a different blouse. When I walked into the room she used as an office, she was conferring with my friend Satterthwaite and another gentleman, plainly in the same line of business, no doubt Henry J. Turner himself. An illustrated catalogue lay open at a full-color picture of what was probably the firm's most expensive coffin.

"Mr. Gates?" Miss DeLong said.

"I'd like to talk to you privately," I said.

"I'm busy. Is it important?"

"It's important."

"Then perhaps these gentlemen wouldn't mind—?"

"Certainly not," Mr. Turner said.

"No, indeedy," Mr. Satterthwaite said.

She came out in the hall with me. "It really has to be only a minute. I have a thousand things to take care of, literally." She smiled. "It was stupid of the lieutenant to think he could keep you out."

"I don't think it was all his idea," I said. "That's why I want to see Mr. Pope."

Her eyebrows went up, though not very far. "About those knockout drops in the coffee. Yes, I heard about it, Mr. Gates, and don't scowl at me. I'm not at all sure it didn't happen. What half convinced me is the coffee pot. Who put it away? Not one of the maids. She would have picked up the champagne bottle and the empty glass, and she would have emptied the ashtrays. But how do you expect Mr. Pope to help you?"

"He can call off his dogs."

"You think Lieutenant Minturn will lie down when Mr. Pope whistles?"

"He doesn't have to whistle. All he has to do is pucker."

"Perhaps you're right," she said, "not that I think there's anything reprehensible about wanting to protect our privacy until the funeral is over. After that we can take care of ourselves. How would you go about proving that somebody doped your coffee? I don't want to seem unsympathetic, but people were streaming in and out of the kitchen last night in droves, few of them sober."

"Were you?"

"I was the exception. I've been reading the newspaper story, and I can see how it would make you wince. But would it have any lasting effect?"

"It won't last until the year 2000," I said, "but neither will I. I lose my insurance company business automatically. I can stand that. Not cheerfully, but I can stand it. My big problem is the cops. I need their respect to operate. Not respect, exactly, but they have to look on me as a professional. Most of the cops I know have a pretty primitive sense of humor, and they're going to think this is the funniest thing since silent pictures. I'll have to take a certain amount of ribbing. I could stand that too, but when my sources in the department dry up, I'm finished. I'm a one-man agency. I'm close to the cliff as it is."

She gave me a sober appraisal. "So I can tell Mr. Pope that you don't mean to let it drop?"

"How can I? You can also tell him that Junior is acting very jittery. He and a couple of friends just took me down to the swimming pool and tried to beat some sense into me."

"That was silly of Dick," she said, frowning. "How is he?"

"Physically he's fine."

"I don't think I'll tell him about that unless I have to. I won't promise, but I'll try. You can wait in my office."

The undertakers looked up as I came in. Mr. Satterthwaite said accusingly, "She hadn't been trying to get me on the phone at all."

"I know," I said. "I was lying."

I saw the early edition of a New York afternoon paper on Miss DeLong's desk. I took it to the window. My name is easy to spell, and they had it spelled correctly, I was sorry to see. Minturn was quoted at length. By the time I finished with the front page and followed the story to page five I was feeling my bruises.

Miss DeLong was gone ten minutes. Mr. Turner and Mr. Satterthwaite fidgeted in silence. She opened the door and beckoned.

"He'll see you, Mr. Gates. But you won't stay long? I probably don't need to say that, because he's perfectly capable of kicking you out."

We went to the stairs. The gathering in the living room had grown in size as more friends and neighbors came in to pay their respects, watch the police at work and drink the Popes' liquor. Some were probably left over from the wedding. Except for the time of day and the high-necked dresses, it might have been a cocktail party instead of a wake.

Miss DeLong was walking quickly, a step or two ahead of me. I didn't know where she fitted into the net of relationships in this house, but I didn't let that interfere with my appreciation of one of the nicest sights afforded by modern civilization—a good-looking girl going upstairs in high heels and a tight skirt. At the top of the stairs she looked around. I don't know if she was pleased by my attention, but she was aware of it. She smoothed her black hair.

We passed an open bedroom. Minturn was sitting on a lady's chaise-longue, looking suspiciously at an open notebook. I recognized the expression, having seen it on the faces of other cops the morning after a killing: he wanted to make sure he hadn't forgotten anything obvious before he went home.

"Excuse me a minute," I said to Miss DeLong, and stepped into the room. "Is this where it happened?"

Minturn's face darkened. "*Gates!* Goddam it, it's beginning to seem that you're really hunting for it."

He snapped the notebook shut and started to heave himself to his feet. Miss DeLong remarked coolly from the doorway, "Mr. Pope wants to see him."

Minturn, halfway up, paused for an instant. To sit down again would have been undignified, so he continued to straighten. Then he had nothing to do but watch me as I looked at the dressing table and the safe, which was still open, and poked into the closet. There was nothing to see, but I stayed long enough to make my point.

"Interesting," I said.

I went back to the corridor. Miss DeLong knocked lightly at the next door. When a voice called to come in, she opened the door and let me go in alone.

It was an office and bedroom combined. Mr. Pope was sitting in the angle of an L-shaped desk. On it I saw several bundles of letters, an untouched lunch tray, a half-filled bottle of whiskey and numerous bottles of pills, probably manufactured by his own company. He was wearing tinted glasses, a kind of smoking jacket, out at the elbows, with a dark scarf knotted around his neck. His sparse gray hair was neatly parted.

"Sit down, Gates. Scotch?"

"Thanks," I said, moving a side-chair closer to the desk.

"Help yourself. There's no ice."

There was also only one glass, and he was drinking out of that. He waved toward the bathroom.

"There's probably one in there."

I found a toothbrush glass, rinsed it out and poured Scotch into it.

"My doctor forbids me the consolations of whiskey," Mr. Pope said. "But in some ways today is exceptional. I suppose a certain amount of drinking is going on downstairs?"

"That's the way it seemed to me," I said. "Nobody offered me any."

"Let us be charitable. They've come to find out if there is anything they can do. Yes, there is something they can do, but I'm afraid they wouldn't thank me for telling them. I want no part of it. Two of my sisters are down there. They can pass the cheese tidbits."

He studied me as I drank. I studied him at the same time, but there is little point in studying somebody wearing dark glasses. All I could see was a small image of myself in each lens.

"My secretary tells me you're going to be a problem," he said.

"Not necessarily. I just want permission to ask a few questions."

"So far I understand that the natives have been rather unfriendly? And apparently you think I dropped a hint or two to Lieutenant Minturn?"

"Didn't you?"

"It wasn't necessary. Minturn is an intelligent officer. He is satisfied with what he takes to be the facts. So am I. I see no profit in pursuing it any further. Neither does he. But I believe you disagree?"

"Damn right I disagree."

"And in addition to your other difficulties, you have had a set-to with my son?"

"He asked me not to tell you about it."

"From that I can guess how it went. Dick has never been lucky in his attempts at self-assertion. I believe Miss DeLong is right, you will be a hard man to ignore. But I'm still not sure exactly what you want."

"Didn't she tell you? I'd like to find out who was working with Moran. And it won't be enough to find out. I have to get it in the papers."

"Are you under any legal pressure? Has anybody threatened to sue you for negligence or revoke your license?"

"It's been mentioned. I don't think it's serious because there wasn't any loss. This is just something I have to do if I want to go on being a private detective."

Mr. Pope rattled his fingers against the desk. "And you do want to go on being a private detective?"

"I think so. I don't know of any other job where you meet so many peculiar people."

He swirled whiskey around in his glass, admired it against the light, and drank some of it. "Miss DeLong made a tentative suggestion. In the pharmaceutical business, as you probably know, dog eats dog. My company maintains a so-called trade research department which sees to it that we are never unpleasantly surprised when one of our competitors brings out a new product. Would work of that kind interest you?"

"It might," I said, "if you gave me a thirty-year contract. I doubt if you will. In six months, after things have cooled off here, I think I'd be unemployed."

He went on rattling his fingers. He was probably looking at me, but because of the dark glasses I couldn't be sure. "And if I ask Lieutenant Minturn to assign me a trooper with orders to arrest you on sight for trespass, how will you proceed?"

"I'll check it at the other end, through Moran."

He leaned forward. "Gates, I am strongly tempted to—"

I broke in. "Before *you* start threatening me, Mr. Pope, don't you see how it looks? Press on it some more and even Minturn may get it. You people are covering up for somebody. I don't care about that— I'm not the Lone Ranger. But you know my problem. Think of some reasonable out and I'll go away and leave you alone."

"I can't think of any," he said after a moment. "Can you?"

"Just the obvious one. Let me look around and see what I turn up."

He sighed. "Then if I am to have any control over you at all, I'll have to hire you. Have another drink."

"No, thanks. I haven't had breakfast yet. Hire me to do what?"

He took his time. "Is there any possibility that you can respect a confidence, Gates?"

"There's a faint possibility," I said. "I'm not very talkative."

He listened to the pleasant sound made by whiskey as it leaves the neck of a bottle and falls into a glass.

"I wonder what delusions you have about the relationship between Lieutenant Minturn and myself. I happen to own a substantial property in this county. I admit to playing golf occasionally with people who have political influence. But this is a capital case. Two people have died, and if you think that Minturn would close down an investigation unless he was completely satisfied with what he had found, you are mistaken. He reconstructs the crime rather simply. Moran stole my wife's jewels, then went down to the library to steal my daughter's. He was shot to death, the loot was recovered. But one thing I didn't mention to the police. There was more than jewelry in the safe in my wife's room. There was seventy-five thousand dollars in cash."

Chapter 7

He mentioned the sum casually, as though only a social misfit would neglect to keep a small amount of cash around the house for an emergency, such as having to pay the paper boy.

"Why didn't you tell Minturn?" I said.

"He didn't ask me." He hesitated. "I am having difficulties with the income-tax people. My lawyers are in the middle of some delicate negotiations right now, and my possession of such a sum in currency might be misunderstood. I'm hoping that Minturn won't get wind of it."

"How did you keep it, in loose bills?"

"In two large envelopes. A few thousand-dollar bills, the rest hundreds. Nobody knew it was there but my wife and myself."

"And you want me to get it back?"

"Without letting anybody know it was there, if possible. I will pay your regular fees and expenses, plus ten percent of any amount you recover."

I must have looked surprised. Seventy-five hundred dollars was a large fee for me. He said gently, "So you won't be tempted to turn the case over to Internal Revenue for the ten percent they pay informers."

That was a nice touch. "I accept," I said promptly.

"And now that you're a client, can I ask you a few questions?"

He took a moment before answering that, which was one of the easy ones. "You'll start drawing expenses as of now. Don't be in too much of a hurry. This is a bad day. I'm not thinking too clearly."

"I want to get that money back before anybody starts paying bills with it. You probably have some idea who took it?"

He spread his hands. "Not the slightest."

"How long has it been in the house?"

"That I can't say with any precision. I make a practice of keeping a certain amount available, sometimes more, sometimes less."

"Even your secretary didn't know about it?"

"I'm quite sure she didn't."

"How long has she worked for you?"

"Three years. Nearer four. But before you go any further, I can assure you that she had nothing to do with it. Put it out of your mind."

"Does she work for you in the city too?"

He put his hands on the desk. "I told you to put it out of your mind."

"That's what you told me," I said. "I don't know why it is; but whenever I ask a simple question, people either go off like a Roman candle or they get very correct. It was Miss DeLong who suggested that I might want some coffee last night. She passed the waitress on the stairs. It may not mean anything, but how can I put her out of my mind until I know more about her?"

He breathed in and out several times before telling

himself to relax. "I'll give you a comprehensive answer, and get it out of the way. Mrs. Pope has been in increasingly poor health. After her second heart attack I rearranged my work so I could do more of it at home. I needed a part-time secretary and a part-time house-keeper, and Miss DeLong asked for the job. At the time she was a typist in the executive pool, at half the salary she now earns. She works two or three hours a day for me. The rest of the time she manages the staff, plans menus and so on."

"And she doesn't live in?"

"She could if she wished, of course. She prefers to maintain an apartment in White Plains. Surely that exhausts the subject of Miss DeLong?"

"All right, Mr. Pope. Now I'd like to ask you about Shelley Hardwick. I understand she was engaged to Dick?"

He circled the question before deciding it was safe to answer. "Here again I fail to see a connection. Yes, she was. My feeling about the engagement is that Dick is well out of it. Shelley is one of my daughter's closest friends. Mrs. Pope and I both tried not to let Dick realize how we felt, but it was obvious that she wasn't suited to him at all. Perhaps they are too much alike. They seem to goad each other on, as though in compe-tition to see which can think of the wildest, the most outrageous and irresponsible—no, that makes it sound romantic. To put it prosaically, Dick's worst scrapes have been ones he and Shelley got into together. That's why I thank God they've broken up at last."

"What kind of scrapes?"

He made a groping gesture. "I see you're not a reader of the New York tabloids."

I stood up. I could think of several other things I ought to know, but they would have to wait. "That's all for now. Do you want to give me a five-hundred-dollar retainer?"

"Of course."

He took out a checkbook and wrote me a check.

"I'll show this to Minturn," I said, waving it to dry the ink. "If you see him, tell him I'm not one of the bad guys any more."

"That's unnecessary. Lieutenant Minturn is sensitive to small changes in the atmosphere. You understand that I want anything you find brought to me first, Mr. Gates. Anything at all that bears on the missing money."

"Sure," I said. "That's the big thing you're buying with this five hundred bucks."

He may have given me a sharp look but again it was wasted on me because of the dark glasses. He was pouring himself another drink when I left.

I went back downstairs without meeting anybody and knocked on the door of Anna DeLong's office. She called to me to come in.

The undertakers were gone. She was at her desk, and Dick Pope was sitting across the room, hunched forward, hands between his legs. He looked up sullenly.

"What did he say?"

"He said you shouldn't try to beat me up any more. I'm looking for Minturn."

"He went back to the barracks," Miss DeLong said. "I think he was afraid you'd want him to apologize."

Dick got up and went out, coming down too emphatically on his heels. The red patch on each cheekbone had widened. Apparently he had been taking some more of the tranquilizing medicine that sells for six dollars a fifth.

"That seems to have been quite a skirmish in the bathhouse," she said. "Sonny is up and about, but Binge Palmer may have to go into a cast, as I know you'll be sorry to hear. Did Mr. Pope succeed in hiring you?"

I sat on a corner of her desk. "I'm not hard to hire. All you have to do is offer me money. How does his tax case stand?"

She had a long sharpened pencil in one hand. She reversed it so the eraser end was down.

"I'd better let him answer the financial questions. But there's one thing I would like to say." She reversed the pencil again. "Go easy on Dick, Mr. Gates."

"Did he tell you I've been picking on him?"

"No, he didn't try to pretty anything up. He doesn't mind feeling guilty about things, in fact he rather enjoys it. And his motives were good. The way it turned out was a bad blow to him. This friend of his, Binge, has done a lot of boasting about the skills he picked up as a Marine, and Sonny was quite a ferocious hockey player in school, I understand. Poor Dick is quite crushed."

I started to say something, but checked it in time, seeing that she was serious.

"I'm not asking you to let him out of anything," she said. "Do what you have to do. But he's a little breakable right now, and I don't want him to be hurt." She looked away and added, "I'm quite fond of Dick."

I said carefully, "Does this have anything to do with the broken engagement?"

She came down too hard on the point of her pencil, and it snapped. "Dick should never have thought about getting married to anybody. He has too many things to work out first."

I waited, but when she didn't go on I said, "Tell him to go easy on me, too. I'm feeling a little breakable myself. Now I'd like to take you over some of the same ground you've probably already covered with the cops. Working for Mr. Pope, did you ever put anything in the safe in his wife's room?"

No, she hadn't. Her replies to my next few questions were equally brief and abstracted. When she volunteered that she was fond of Dick Pope, who was a few years younger than she was, recently engaged to someone else, and in my opinion quite a mess, I had expected a little more frankness, but that was apparently my confidence for the day.

The wedding presents had been packed and carted off to a bank vault, and Davidson and I used the library, working hard for a few hours without accomplishing much. No one could throw any light on how the knockout medicine had found its way into my coffee, or how the coffee pot had found its way from the library back to the kitchen. No one had known of Leo Moran's existence before the moment he was shot, or if they had they wouldn't admit it.

"It's beginning to blur, Ben," Davidson said as he took one of the maids to the door. "You slept all night. I didn't. Let's go home."

"O.K.," I said.

"What did I hear you say?" he asked suspiciously. "O.K.?"

"Are we making any headway here?"

"I doubt it, but I haven't been listening for the last couple of hours. I've been wondering why we don't talk to Shelley Hardwick."

"She's next. I'm going to give her a ride to town."

"If you want her to talk sense you'd better hurry up, Ben. The last time I saw her she was well on the way to Happy Junction."

"Oh, God." I rubbed out my cigar in the ashtray. "I want that girl to communicate. Is Minturn still talking to you?"

"He's a little cool. If I tried to get into the barracks, I don't think he'd actually throw me out. But, Ben—"

"I want to know what's come in on Moran. Then could you come back and keep an eye on Dick Pope?"

He looked at me unhappily. "I'll have to take a couple of bennies to stay awake. I wouldn't say he's the type that goes to bed early."

"Tail him if he goes anywhere. He's been pushing the booze all day, and that shouldn't be hard. I'll leave word with Mrs. Rooney at the office where you can reach me."

I phoned for a cab and looked for Shelley Hardwick. I found her in the living room, not far from the impro-vised bar. Two stern-faced women in black, probably

Pope's sisters, had set up a kind of receiving line. I bypassed it and picked my way among the mourners, who were gathered in awkward groups, drinking and making conversation until they had been there long enough so it would be polite to leave, or had drunk enough so they wouldn't want to. One of the few people who seemed to be enjoying this curious ceremony was the tall youth named Sonny. Wearing a head bandage, he was talking in a low enthusiastic voice to Shelley, who had given him the crack on the head that had made the bandage necessary. She listened with a dreamy smile. Her suitcase was on the floor at her feet.

"But the whole point is," Sonny said, "that dreams are connected in a hell of a complex way with the sub-conscious memory of the race. That's where Jung busted up with the old man. And Fromm—"

"Shelley," I said.

She looked up from her drink, which she was holding in both hands, so no one could take it away from her. "Are we ready?"

"I left my car in Prosper," I said. "A taxi ought to be here in a couple of minutes."

"Do you two know each other?" she said. "This is— That's right. You did meet, didn't you?"

"How do you do?" Sonny said, and continued, "And where Fromm differs from the other boys—"

"Sonny, go get Ben a Scotch. Don't tell Dick who wants it. He's probably still nursing a grudge."

I picked up her suitcase. "I won't have time for a drink. Bring yours, you can finish it outside."

She was open to any reasonable suggestion, and she

considered this reasonable until Sonny topped it with an even more reasonable one—that we go some place where they had dancing. It took me ten minutes to argue her out of that, and by then I was thinking of asking for the loan of her high-heeled shoe. Sonny wandered off. We received some disapproving looks on our way to the door, for which I couldn't blame the people. We were obviously neither of us in mourning for anybody.

Dick overtook us in the hall. "Leaving?"

"Ben's driving me," Shelley said. She patted me under the left arm. "And he carries a gun, too. I felt it last night. So nothing can happen to me, isn't that nice?"

"Shell, I have something that belongs to you. Do you want it?"

"What?"

He grinned. "Have a drink with me and I'll tell you."

"Oh, you're so brilliant," she said. "But not quite brilliant enough. I'll come out for the funeral tomorrow and you can give it to me then."

She pulled me by the sleeve and we walked away.

"What was that all about?" I said.

She giggled. "Haven't you realized by now that I'm a very mysterious girl? Don't bother your head, Ben. Richardson Pope, Jr. makes almost no sense the first thing in the morning, and he makes less and less as the day goes on."

The taxi was waiting. The driver and I recognized each other. He was the one I had told to wait outside Hilda Faltermeier's that morning.

"Hey—"

"I'll pay you," I said. "I'll pay you."

"You're damn well told you'll pay me."

So I paid him. I thought his figure was a bit high, but from this point on I was spending expense account money, which can't be compared with regular money.

As we made the turn at the foot of the drive, Shelley swayed against me, putting her head on my shoulder and one hand against my gun. She said something like, "Ummm." Then she said, "That was quite a transformation. You were the world's most unpopular man this morning, and now everybody seems to think you're great. What happened?"

"I won them over," I said.

"Was that my lipstick you were wearing, incidentally?"

"Yeah."

"I thought I recognized the shade." She gave another low laugh. "I really must have craved that diamond bracelet. I thought afterward that I should have told the trooper I was responsible for the champagne bottle and so on. Then I don't know, I got sidetracked."

"Never mind," I said. "Men are never supposed to claim they've been raped."

She drew back. "Did we—"

"No, no. Figure of speech. How much do you remember of what happened last night? Why did Junior knock you down?"

She pulled back all the way, leaving my gun alone. "He knocked me down! Why, the son of a bitch! What did he do that for?"

"You made some kind of cryptic remark about White Plains. That's all I know."

"Well, that accounts for part of it," she said. "I thought I'd passed out, and it scared me. If I'm going to start blacking out at my age I'll have to stop drinking, and that would be a shame. Nothing interesting ever happens to me when I'm sober."

"Do you remember going to bed?"

"Vaguely. It seems to me I got upstairs under my own steam. It also seems to me that I played tag with somebody in the hall, Binge or somebody, but it's all confused. I'd make a horrible witness if I had to testify. I had an embarrassing session with Lieutenant Minturn. I've never seen a man so disgusted with anybody." A giggle broke through. "Did you notice those teeth? They *glared* at me, Ben."

Another thought struck her, and she looked at me more closely.

I said, "No, mine are my own."

"That's a relief."

"Over there, driver," I said.

He halted the cab in front of the supermarket and I paid him another fare. I took Shelley to my Buick.

"Be right with you. I've got to make a couple of phone calls."

There was an outside booth at the edge of the parking area. I dialed several numbers before I got the one I wanted, and then I was twice given the wrong extension and the waiting cost me another dime. Finally a man named Darcy answered. I told him my name.

"I'd better make sure I've got the right extension this time," I said. "This is the Intelligence Unit? You're in charge of preparing income-tax prosecutions in the Southern District?"

"That is correct."

"I'm working with the State Police. We're interested in Richardson Pope. Can you tell me the status of his evasion case at the moment?"

"Who did you say you were?"

I went over that again and gave him time to write it down. Then he said, "I'm sorry, Mr. Gates, we're not permitted to give out that information."

I made a rude noise. "In other words, there isn't any case?"

"You might make that inference," he said cautiously. "But I would like to point out something. Naturally we will now give Mr. Pope's recent returns a most careful audit. If there is anything amiss, you can rest assured that we'll find it. So if you have any information, why don't you bring it in? You may not know that the Treasury is authorized to pay a so-called intelligence fee of—"

I assured him that I knew about it and hung up, not really disappointed to find that my new client, who had told me that his lawyers were negotiating with the income-tax people, had been lying to me. Occasionally that happens, and when it does I try not to let it make me cynical.

Chapter 8

While I had the booth I put in a personal call to Sonia Petrofsky at a New York newspaper. Sonia, an old friend of mine, is the daytime secretary of a night-blooming personal-item columnist, whose working life is spent among press agents and celebrities in various Manhattan saloons. Much of my practice is among the same class of people, which gives us something in common. She has the memory of UNIVAC, the energy of Rosalind Russell, and great charm. We would have been married long ago except that she considers me too young for her. She is fifty-nine.

"Ben!" she exclaimed when I said hello. "I've been expecting to hear from you since I saw the papers."

"I couldn't use the phone where I was."

"I've got the folders right here. This is quite a mess you've got yourself into, Ben, and it doesn't sound like you. In fact, it sounds so much not like you that it probably didn't happen. Could I be right?"

"Sonia," I said, "it's nice to hear your voice, believe me. I was robbed. The question is, can I prove it? So far the answer is no. What folders did you get out?"

"Richardson Pope, father and son. Go ahead?"

"Go ahead."

"Well, the father seems to be pretty overprotected by his public relations people. He gives speeches. He gets elected to things. But there's not much here that wasn't mimeographed first. His namesake is something else again. This boy has probably given ulcers to several generations of his daddy's press agents. Every time he gets in trouble the company's name gets in the paper. He gets in trouble often. You'll probably want to see these with your own eyes."

"Give me a quick view from the air."

"Here's a slight case of statutory rape. Fifteen-year-old girl, charges withdrawn after getting the necessary newspaper space, no doubt indicating a tidy cash settlement. He ran a Ferrari into a pole and killed the girl who was with him. For that they took away his driver's license for six months. Fight on the sidewalk outside of 21, like the street fights in East Harlem except that this was between Yales and Princetons. Our boy's role was a little puzzling because he's been kicked out of both Yale and Princeton. Maybe everybody turned on him—he spent three weeks in Harkness."

"I hope there's something about a fire?"

"Oh, yes. Let me see—three months ago. A recreation building burned down on the Prosper estate. Mr. and Mrs. Pope were away and Junior was giving a party. Correction, a *wild* party. What made the fire noteworthy was that a man was burned to death. You read about it, Ben."

"It must have been when I was working on that proxy fight," I said. "Did it make the *Wall Street Journal?*"

"Probably not. The man's name was Samuel Pattberg, but I don't think he was important enough for

the *Wall Street Journal.* A self-reliant small business-
man, the kind that made America great. He handled
dirty movies."

I heard a faint click, as though one tumbler in a
complicated lock was falling into place. But it was only
the operator, asking for more money. I gave her some,
and said to Sonia, "He was showing movies at Junior's
party?"

"Flaming youth, Ben. After he ran off the films to
the enjoyment of all, the party moved on. Dancing.
Drinking. Swimming in the moonlight. Fertility rites
amid the poison ivy. You know what wild parties are
like—the Ten Commandments are fractured rather
freely, I believe. Everybody forgot about Pattberg.
He'd been paid. The idea was that he'd gone home.
Actually he was having a little one-man wild party in
the projection booth, locked up with a bottle of hard
liquor and all those cans of film. Along around three in
the morning he wanted a cigarette, and by then he was
too drunk to read the no-smoking signs. Pornographic
film is just as combustible as the ordinary kind, if not
more so. Goodbye, Mr. Pattberg. The only thing the
firemen were able to save was the swimming pool."

"There's no doubt about how it started?"

"I guess not. A big bang, and the place went up.
They didn't know Pattberg was missing until they
counted the cars and found one left over. At first
Junior insisted they'd been looking at old Charlie
Chaplin shorts, but Pattberg was traced through his
registration. The police knew what he really dis-
tributed, and it wasn't Charlie Chaplin."

I had been keeping an eye on the Buick through the glass wall of the booth. The front door opened.

I said hastily, "I have to go now, Sonia. Thanks. I'll be in touch."

I missed the bracket with the phone, and left it dangling. I got back to the Buick while Shelley was reaching into the back seat for her suitcase.

"Sorry that took so long," I said.

"Oh," she said, "I was getting a little dehydrated. Don't you think a fast drink would be nice?"

I looked at my watch and pretended to consider. "Maybe we'd better get on in."

I waited till we were on the parkway before I brought up the fire. She swung toward me sharply.

"Why do you want to know about *that*? There can't be any connection with what happened last night."

"There's a dim kind of connection," I said. "Leo Moran was arrested once for sending obscene matter through the mails. That's almost the only thing we know about him so far."

She made a low gargling sound. "Somebody's been telling you about those movies, I see. Don't call them obscene. That sounds too dignified." She sat back. "Do you know what I thought you were going to say? That you'd found out that Dick started the fire."

I looked away from the road.

"But don't quote me, for God's sake," she said.

"He set fire to the building to kill Pattberg?"

"No! My God, no. That part was an accident. Dick

may have his little quirks, but he wouldn't deliberately— At least, I don't think—"

"Did Dick know Pattberg before?"

"Neither of us did. It was all arranged by phone. He came out a couple of days earlier to look things over, and that was the first time we set eyes on him. And what a repulsive little man! I suppose you have to be repulsive, or it wouldn't occur to you to go into that business. But he overdid it, I thought. It wasn't a hot day but he was sweating, and for some reason even his sweat didn't seem real. It looked like whatever it is actors use. That's why nobody could get worked up about it when he was killed. He hadn't seemed to be very alive in the first place. He was alive *legally,* I admit that. Dick gave him some money in advance, which was a mistake, because he was drunk and sleepy when he showed up the night of the party. He had trouble getting the reels on the projector, and somebody had to do the focusing for him. He ran one reel backward and upside down—quite an interesting effect, as a matter of fact."

She gave me a curiously shy look. "It's probably an old story to you, but it was my first exposure to the art form, and I don't care if it never happens again. I let it get under my skin. It was so damned crude! I don't mean just what the actors were doing. Everything. And don't grin at me, damn it. It wasn't funny."

"But you stayed to the end?"

"How did you know?" she said bitterly. "Yes, and so did everybody, but we all did some squirming. Even

Dick was embarrassed, though naturally he wouldn't admit it. He kept applauding and making dumb remarks, but he knew it was a mistake. That's really why I think he set the fire. This is a little psychiatric, but I think he wanted to get rid of anything that would remind him of those gruesome movies."

"Where was everybody?"

"In swimming. Most of this didn't come out at the time, which is just as well. After that movie fiasco, the party never really got on its feet. It was just—I don't know, blah. Maybe Dick was trying too hard. It was a big disappointment, because his parents hadn't let him have any parties since he smashed up a car last year. People began going home. Then the moon came up and he insisted we all go for a swim. *Au naturel,* naturally. In the raw, to put it in English."

She was looking straight ahead. "It seemed a little childish, but Dick was determined. There's no electricity in the bathhouse, so we got undressed in the recreation building, the girls in the lounge, the boys in the billiard room. All our clothes went up in the fire, which was probably part of the point. It made the party a huge success."

I glanced at her again and she said defensively, "As parties go."

"Dick went in too?"

"Yes, but the lights were out. He could slip out of the pool and nobody would know the difference. So we wanted entertainment? He'd give us entertainment. What could be more diverting than a big fire at three in the morning? We got the volunteer firemen out of bed and *they* enjoyed it. I don't know if you've ever been to a fire in the country—it's like a carnival. People come from all over. And this one had a novel touch. We were splashing around in the pool, shrieking like a lot of boy-girl campers when the counselors are off at a meeting. We scrambled out and grabbed towels, and after that there was the problem of getting something else on before the firemen got there. We rushed into the house and began going through closets. We ended up in some pretty peculiar outfits. The firemen must have known we'd been in swimming, but thank God there was no way of telling that we'd been in minus suits. It was all very exciting, and the people who went home early sulked for weeks. When we found out about Pattberg it was a little less gay. Not much, but a little. The State Police asked a lot of questions. But Pattberg had been Pattberg, and nobody really cared. The insurance man was tougher because money was involved. He didn't want to pay unless he had to. He did, finally.

"You didn't tell him you thought Dick started the fire?"

"No! Nobody did. Not everybody at the party was really wild about him, but nobody wanted to get him into that kind of trouble. And what could we say? We saw him dancing around with a wild light in his eyes. Maybe that was the pride of authorship and maybe it was plain animal spirits. But there's one other thing that makes me think he did it. His father got an analyst for him afterward. Before that he was famous for not believing in it."

She lit a cigarette. "Ben, is it true that you're working for him? Mr. Pope?"

"I have his check in my pocket. But why not tell me what you wanted me to do? I might have some time."

"It, was just a daydream, Ben. I might as well make up my mind, Dick and I are kaput. And it's not such a terrible tragedy."

I waited. If there was enough pressure behind it she would tell me without any prodding.

"Oh, hell," she said. "I'm not sure about anything any more. God knows he's hard to get along with, and he hasn't been getting any easier. That fight last night was typical. But we always managed to make up until Anna DeLong came on the scene. I keep telling myself that Dick's of legal age, and if he can't button his own clothes it's none of my business. But I know one thing. This goddam analyst is steering him her way! And she's wrong for him! I'm not just saying that because I'm a jealous bitch. She really is. She's as cold as ice. She's years older than he is. She must be twenty-seven, anyway. He's always broke these days— he even owes *me* money—but he's going to be on the check-cashing end of a perfectly lovely trust arrangement before too long, and that's why her glittering eye is fixed on him. There's something very, very fishy about that girl."

"In what way?"

She turned eagerly. "I know you're going to discount about ninety percent of this, but why did she take that job unless she was setting her sights on the son and heir? She worked in Mr. Pope's office in the city. She must know his financial position. People are always going to get sick and need medicine, and those dividends are going to keep on coming in. Another thing she must have known from following Dick's career in the papers—he's a sitting duck. All she had to do was wear tailored suits and look efficient and he'd fall in her lap."

"Don't tell me she doesn't really need to wear glasses?"

"I wouldn't put it past her! Well, I admit I was irked when they started having those long intimate conversations, but if she'd been right for him I would have bowed out gracefully. May the best girl win, and all that crap. But it's terribly unhealthy, Ben. It really is. He needed a mother once, but not now, for God's sake. And she's such a *phony* phony. Don't tell me anybody can be *that* unruffled in the bosom of the Pope family. She's either beyond human feelings or she's putting on an act. That's what I wanted to hire you to find out. What does anybody know about her? She has a biography, but it's all in one dimension, and it doesn't convince me. She says she went to the University of Michigan. Now I can't take her off in a corner and ask her what class she was in and what did she take up and did she or didn't she graduate. But I've run into three separate people who were at Michigan about when she would have been unless she was a child prodigy, and they never heard of her. Well, it's a big place. But I thought if I could show her up for a fakearoo, maybe Dick could see for himself that she doesn't really care about him, she's going for the trust fund."

I saw a booth ahead, and slowed to pay the nagging little toll.

"It's easy to find out if she went to Michigan. Write them a letter."

"What good would it do? She could talk her way out of that. It would have to be something like serving a prison term for selling abortions. Nothing that woman could do would surprise me! But I've been saving something, Ben, that shows she may not be quite the *Ladies' Home Journal* character she pretends to be. It may throw some light on your problem, too. Now listen."

She took two quick puffs at her cigarette. I was listening.

"Last Saturday night we went to a dance at the country club. Dick and I. We were still drinking martinis at midnight, which will give you the idea. Dick took it into his empty head to repeat a few things his father and mother had been telling him about me. They never liked me, for some nonrational reason. I knew this, but I didn't enjoy hearing it from my fiancé, who's no candidate for beatification himself. You know the kind of thing. I've got a reputation for not being too celibate, or whatever the word is." She glanced at me. "And I couldn't care less. What was I supposed to do, sit there like a perfect lady? I answered back. I've been known to disgrace myself at that country club, but this time I managed to keep it genteel. I didn't throw anything. I made him mad, I'm happy to say. He walked out and climbed into his Mercury. I thought I'd better find out where he was going, so I swiped somebody's car. Dick was weaving all over the road at seventy miles an hour, which they don't recommend at driving school. How he made it to White Plains I don't know, but he made it. He pulled up in front of a big apartment house. I was right behind him. If he'd been taking a higher proportion of vermouth in his martinis he couldn't have missed me. He left the Merc double-parked and went in. I saw a phone booth, and just to make absolutely sure I looked up Anna DeLong's address. That was who it was, all right."

I'd already made that entry in my chart of connections. I made a sound to show I was interested, and asked, "How long did you wait?"

"Now be patient, Ben," she said. "So far it's not too surprising. Dick had his feelings hurt and ran off to Mother so she could kiss it and make it well. Meanwhile, what had Mother been up to? That's something I'd been wondering about. It's more convenient for a housekeeper to live in, and the Popes have plenty of extra rooms. Why commute to White Plains, of all places? I was trying to make up my mind what to do. Go back to the dance and forget about it? Ring the doorbell? Stamp my foot and scream? Then a man came out of the building."

"Moran?" I said quickly.

"You spoiled it!" she cried. "Couldn't you wait a minute? Yes, that's who it was, but I didn't know it till I saw his picture in the paper today. He looked as though he'd put his clothes on in a hurry. I don't know if his shoes were untied or not. That's the impression I got. He saw Dick's Mercury. It's a white convertible, and parked that way you couldn't very well not see it. Dick had left the keys in the ignition, which was like him. Moran took the keys out, juggled them for a minute, and then threw them away, threw them as far away as he could. I had what I thought was a bright idea. He must know something about Anna's private life, so why shouldn't I go in for a little counter-intelligence? I opened the door of the booth as he went past and said, 'Don't I know you?—Aren't you a friend of Anna DeLong's?'—something like that. He was big and black-haired and good-looking, and before I could count to three I knew I shouldn't have spoken to him. I was wearing a party dress. Dick had on a white coat and black tie. That meant we'd come from the same place."

She threw her cigarette out the window. "He looked me over, and by that time I was sure of just one thing—I was going to have some trouble. It was a quiet neighborhood and a quiet time of night. His hands kept opening and shutting, and they were big hands. When he asked me who I was and who Dick was, I told him. He wanted to know how Dick had met Anna, and I told him that. Dick had routed him out of a nice comfortable bed, and I was pretty sure he was going to take justice into his own hands and get a little revenge with me. But not at all. He told me I was going back to the dance without disturbing the happy couple. And that's all that happened. He got his car and followed me all the way. When I turned in at the country club he honked twice and drove on. If you can make any sense out of that, you're welcome to it."

I was still trying to make sense of it when I stopped in front of her apartment house on Central Park West. A doorman in uniform hurried across the sidewalk, his money-hand itching.

"Ben, you'll have to eat somewhere," Shelley said. "Why not come up? I'll make you some nice nourishing spaghetti."

"Good evening, Miss Hardwick," the doorman said with a sketchy salute.

"Good evening, John," she said, and went on, "And while the water's coming to a boil we could have some nice nourishing bourbon. Come on, Ben. You'll think of some more questions to ask me."

She touched my sleeve, and I saw a distant glimmer of the same wildness I had seen in her eyes the night before. It made me think of the projection room at Dick Pope's party, filled with explosive material waiting for a spark.

"I could even say please," she said.

"You don't have to go that far. Can I use your phone?"

"They've been threatening to disconnect it, but I think it's still working. John, can you find a parking space for Mr. Gates's car?"

"I'll do my best, Miss Hardwick," he said.

That settled it. I surrendered the Buick, only half-expecting to see it again. In my experience in this part of town, the nearest parking space was somewhere in the upper Bronx.

"He's a magician," Shelley said as we went into the

lobby. "He controls the north side of Seventy-Third from here to Columbus, and on Christmas he's one of the richest men in town."

An elderly elevator operator, even more servile than the doorman, took us up. The apartment, which we reached after a walk down a carpeted hall, had apparently been decorated by a Japanese with a strong yen for the old country.

Shelley kicked off her shoes. "Weird, isn't it? Everything's Japanese but the air-conditioning. It isn't mine. It's easy to borrow apartments in the summer." She pointed out the phone. "The phone book's in English."

She waved and took her suitcase into a bedroom off a low balcony. I went down some steps to the living room. To use the phone I had to sit on the floor. I settled myself on a cushion and dialed my secretary's number.

Mrs. Rooney, a profane, motherly body who is all but disqualified for her profession by her fear of the typewriter, answered breathlessly. "You call at the damnedest times, Mr. Gates. I've got a soufflé in the oven."

"I just want to give you a phone number. Davidson's going to be calling you."

I read her the number on the phone in my hand. After writing it down she said, "People have been trying to reach you. A detective named Joe Josephs. A couple of other cops. Reporters. One or two just people. Butter wouldn't melt in their mouths, the bastards. They wanted to know if they could help, as though the world had come to an end or something. What crime did you commit, after all? You took a couple of drinks. And that's what I told them."

"Thanks, Mrs. Rooney. The soufflé?"

"Christ!"

As soon as I could get the operator's attention I put in a personal call to Anna DeLong at the Popes' number. A maid told the operator that Miss DeLong had left for the day. There was no answer at her White Plains number. That was all right with me; now I could relax.

Shelley brought in two drinks. "Don't get up," she said. "If you get up you'll just have to sit on the floor somewhere else. See if this is the way you like it."

It was plain bourbon, and the ice hadn't been melting long enough to spoil the flavor. Shelley kicked over another cushion.

"I bought a kimono to go with the décor," she said. "I could put it on."

"You look fine," I told her, which was true.

She looked down at me. My head was on a level with her hips; considering everything, which I was doing with my usual attention to detail, it wasn't a bad level to be on. She moved closer. The air between us was highly charged, and I wouldn't have been surprised to hear thunder.

"I'm going to make a short speech," she said. "I know you've been careful not to promise anything, but I have a feeling that things may have changed for the better. I've been worried as hell. All that business with Dick—it's been getting out of hand. I'm glad you're here."

She came down to me slowly, her eyes closing as she passed the focal point. She touched me only with her lips. They moved against mine, and for an instant I felt the promise of her tongue.

She put her drink on the floor. A moment later mine was beside it. Then she came all the way down and moved in against me.

"Don't you want to take off your coat?" she said. "And your tie? I'll help you."

So I took off my coat and my tie. It didn't stop there. And when a girl helps me unbutton my shirt I consider that the least I can do is return the favor. I still didn't know why she was being so hospitable, but there was only one way to find out.

"Or do you want to eat first?" she said after a moment.

"I'm not that hungry."

When the phone rang, a while later, I kicked over my drink. That is one big disadvantage of having everything take place on the floor. Shelley said, "Hell!" and lay still, only her fingertips moving gently. The phone rang again.

"No point in answering," she said. "It's probably not for either of us."

"Probably not."

"And even if it was, they can call back later."

"Much later," I said.

"On the other hand," she said as it rang a third time,

"if we found out it was anything important, we'd feel awfully silly, wouldn't we?"

She picked up the phone as it started to ring again. I heard a man's voice. She made a disgusted face and handed the phone to me.

"Irving?" I said.

"Yeah," he said, "and I've got to make it fast. I have Moran's address. Somebody made him from his picture and called it in." He gave me an address on Riverside Drive. "That's at Ninety-Sixth. Ben, you're still on?"

"Oh, yes."

"I'm going to need some relief. Life is beginning to lose its meaning. Maybe we can make a shift right now, because I seem to have my boy treed."

"Dick?"

"That's right. He drives a pretty loud convertible, and it's been a simple tail, which is lucky for all of us because I'm not up to anything very brainy. I went to sleep twice on the way in, and you don't want to lose me, do you? I can see his car from here, but I'd better get back. You do the phoning. Elmer lives near here— maybe you can get him. I'll be across the street on the Central Park side, and hurry it up, please. It's Central Park West, south of Seventy-Second."

I laughed.

"Ha-ha," Davidson said. "And what's so funny, old man?"

"Central Park West, south of Seventy Second. That's where *I* am."

"Big coincidence," Davidson said. "Then I can go home?"

I made a quick calculation. "Not yet. If he bolts as soon as he sees me, you'll have to stay with him. I'll try to hang onto him. Call Elmer. Phone me when it's set."

The buzzer sounded.

"There he is now."

Chapter 9

I hung up.

"That's Dick," I said. "Does he have a key?"

She scrambled to her feet. "Yes, but I can put on the chain."

I shook my head. I wanted to know what he was after. We had some picking-up to do before we let anybody in. Shelley gathered various discarded articles of clothing and threw them into the bedroom, closing the door. She renewed her lipstick, peering at her reflection in a small mirror, while I was doing what I could to rub off some of the lipstick she had lost. It seemed to me that this was how I had spent a good part of the day.

She put away her tools and threw me a questioning look. I nodded.

The buzzer gave another impatient summons.

"Control yourself, control yourself," Shelley said, and opened the door.

Dick pushed it out of her hand. "It's about time, goddam it. You've got some explaining to do."

He stopped as he saw me. Somebody had sewn a mourning band to his right sleeve, and it didn't go with his manner. With his head lowered and his eyebrows close together, he looked like a bull faced with an enemy in fancy dress, waving a cape. He did everything but paw the ground. Then he turned on Shelley. I was in a position to know exactly what she was wearing, and in spite of the fresh lipstick, it wasn't enough. The blouse was made of some flimsy miracle fabric, and it wasn't sufficiently confining.

"Gates!" Dick said, looking back at me. "How far do I have to travel to get *away* from you?"

He came down the steps. For an instant I thought he was going to hit me, but he remembered in time that he didn't have any friends with him. "Do you know what I'd like to do to you? I'd like to—" He broke off with a disgusted wave of the hand.

Shelley had followed him. "State your business," she said. "I'd offer you a drink, only I know your analyst wouldn't approve."

"You have a funny idea about analysis," he said. He brushed the back of his hand up and down across her breast. "I thought so. No bra. No slip. You needed a friend at court, and what easier way? But you don't know private detectives. A thing like this makes absolutely no difference. It's an episode. Am I right, Gates?"

"Maybe you'd better make him a drink," I said. "I could use one myself. I kicked mine over."

"Listen, Gates," Dick said. "Am I wrong in thinking you're open to any reasonable offer? How much do you want to run down and get a pack of cigarettes?"

"If Shelley wants to talk to you, I'll do it for nothing."

"I don't want to talk to him," she said. "I'd appreciate it if you'd throw him out."

"He can try," Dick said. "He may find it's not so easy." He threw his arms wide. "What do you want out

Get Hard Case Crime by Mail...
And Save 43%!

☐ **YES! Sign me up for the Hard Case Crime Book Club!**

As long as I choose to stay in the club, I will receive every Hard Case Crime book as it is published (generally one each month). I'll get to preview each title for 10 days. If I decide to keep it, I will pay only $3.99* — a savings of 43% off the cover price! There is no minimum number of books I must buy and I may cancel my membership at any time.

Name:

Address:

City / State / ZIP:

Telephone:

E-Mail:

☐ **I want to pay by credit card:** ☐ VISA ☐ MasterCard ☐ Discover

Card #:   Exp. date:

Signature:

Mail this card to:
HARD CASE CRIME BOOK CLUB
1 Mechanic Street, Norwalk, CT 06850-3431

Or fax it to 610-995-9274.
You can also sign up online at www.dorchesterpub.com.

* Plus $2.00 for shipping. Offer open to residents of the U.S. and Canada only. Canadian residents please call 1-800-481-9191 for pricing information.

If you are under 18, a parent or guardian must sign. Terms, prices, and conditions subject to change. Subscription subject to acceptance. Dorchester Publishing reserves the right to reject any order or cancel any subscription.

of me, Gates? I'm serious. That was a lousy deal for you last night, and what I can do to straighten it out, I'll do. The way I understand it, somebody tampered with the coffee, right? And the troopers won't believe it? Well, I was in the kitchen—"

"Dick, don't be a horse's ass," Shelley said.

"Why shouldn't I be in the kitchen?" he said. "I wanted a hot cup of coffee because I had a feeling I was getting too tanked. A guy was filling a little coffee pot. One of the caterer's people—white tie and so on. And he got kind of flustered when I tried to take the pot, he said he had an order for it. I'm willing to sign my name to a goddam affidavit."

"And in return for this," I said, "you'd like me to put on my gun and say good night?"

"That's the deal, boy."

Shelley was frowning at me and shaking her head. Dick said, "Let him make up his own mind, will you, for Christ's sake?"

"Is it true?" I said.

He looked surprised. "I thought we were being practical. You can't have a clear picture of that wedding if you think I know whether or not I went down to the kitchen for coffee."

"If you really want to help—" I said, but Dick interrupted.

"Did I say I wanted to help? I just want a few private words with this bitch. Excuse me. That's no way to talk about our charming hostess. Shell."

She had picked up the glass and was starting for the kitchen. She turned. "What do you want?"

"I don't like to do it in front of an audience," he said, "but if that's the way it has to be, O.K. I made the biggest mistake in my life when I called off our engagement, and I hope it's not too late. Let's turn back the calendar. I've had all day to think about it, and I'm damn near going crazy. Give me a chance, will you?"

"Crud," she said.

"Look at me, I'm down on my knees," he said dramatically, though he remained standing.

"Double crud," she said more emphatically, and went up the stairs.

Dick ran his fingers through his hair in exasperation. He dropped onto a low backless sofa, plunging both hands in his pockets.

"Watch your step with this girl, Gates," he said. "And I do know what I'm talking about, believe me."

"How drunk were you last night?" I said, sitting down across from him, within reach of the phone. "Do you remember the shots?"

Shelley came back with the bottle and glasses filled with ice. She put the glasses on a low table and filled them with bourbon.

"For you, Junior, nothing," she said to Dick, handing me a glass.

"You didn't hear the man's question," Dick said. "Mr. Gates just asked if I heard the shots. You'll be interested to know that I was in the land of dreams. They had to wake me up to tell me the news. They had one hell of a time doing it, too."

"According to you," she said.

"And do you know what I was dreaming about? I

didn't want the troopers to hear about it, but you won't mind if I tell Gates. I was dreaming about that time we took the redhead to Newport. I'm sure it was the redhead because I was dreaming in color. What was her name—Gloria. I give you full credit for that. It was your idea. Quite a weekend."

She said to me, "Now he's trying to embarrass you so you'll leave."

"A little piece of Americana like that wouldn't embarrass Gates," Dick said.

The phone rang. I took it.

Davidson's voice said, "Elmer's in position, Ben, so I'm saying good night."

"What number are you calling?"

"I told him to report to Mrs. Rooney up to midnight, so let her know if you go anywhere."

"Just a moment." I covered the mouthpiece and asked Shelley, "When does your landlord get back?"

"September."

I passed this on to Davidson. He said, "And don't disturb me before nine in the morning."

I put the phone back. Dick was speaking to Shelley in an urgent undertone. She smiled and I heard her say, "You're crazy. Sweet but crazy."

"Whatever it is, let's change the subject," I said. "Dick, what did your mother keep in her safe besides jewelry?"

He stopped breathing, which was all I could expect. "How should I know? I'm only twenty-three."

"Did you ever have occasion to use it?"

"That would be quite an occasion, Gates. You can't

use a combination safe unless you know the combination, and now that Mother is dead nobody knows it but my old man. Not only that, he keeps changing the damn thing."

"Then he keeps something in it?"

"I suppose so, sure, when he brings papers home he doesn't want to leave lying around. Everybody in the drug business has secrets." He looked upward at me through his heavy eyebrows. "I'm beginning to get it. He hired you because something's supposed to be missing? Gates, I'm going to tell you about my father. He's fast and he's tricky. That's his reputation, and he does his best to live up to it. He's been known to tell the truth when it didn't cost him money, but in this case the odds are against it."

"Then why do you think he hired me?"

"Aah," Dick said in disgust. "He just wants you to dig up something to pin on his only son."

I tasted the drink Shelley had given me, and found it the same good bourbon. "How did you hear about this guy Pattberg and his movies?"

He stared at me, and lost some of his high gloss. Turning to Shelley, he said in low deadly tones, "You utter, unmitigated— You'd better watch yourself, or by God I'll—"

He stopped, his hands shaking. Shelley knew him better than I did, and she seemed to be impressed.

He stood up slowly. "Gates, I'm going to ask you once more. I can't explain, but won't you *please* give me a couple of minutes alone with this—this— No, that sounds all wrong. I give you my word of honor—"

"As a gentleman," Shelley put in.

"I give you my word I won't lay a finger on her."

"It's not your finger I'm thinking about," she said.

"Shut up!" he said savagely. "Don't pay attention to her, Gates. You've got yourself to look out for. If I know my old man, and goddam it, I do, he offered you a big fee, but only if you accomplished something. This won't damage you, in fact it may help. But don't ask me how."

"I have to ask you how," I said. "How?"

He looked around in desperation. His eyes fell on my gun harness, hanging from the back of a chair. There was a visible change in his inner chemistry. I watched the change without offering him any advice. The gun was on safety, and I didn't carry a live round in the chamber when I went to a girl's apartment for spaghetti. I would have plenty of time to take it away from him.

He reached that conclusion by himself.

"All I have to say is," he said, "the world certainly seems to be full of sons of bitches. Don't worry about me, Shell. I'll make out."

She pulled back as he reached for her, then stood still and let him touch her cheek.

"Do something special for Gates," he said. "Maybe you can get him to stay all night. Want a suggestion?"

"Maybe I could show him some dirty movies?"

He caressed her cheek lightly, then pulled back his hand as if to slap her. "You'll hear from me."

He went out.

Shelley rubbed her cheek where he had touched

her. "That's a disturbed boy, and I hope he comes to no harm. Let's eat."

"Sure. But then I've got to go."

I went to the window and looked down. I saw Dick explode from the building, walking fast with his head down. The doorman came after him, but Dick waved him away. He had double-parked his Mercury with the lights on and the motor running. The doorman wanted to be paid something for watching it. Dick slammed the door, made an illegal turn and roared north, much too fast. I didn't see Elmer, but I assumed that he was somewhere in the following traffic.

Shelley had come over beside me. "He wasn't fooling," she said quietly. "He'll be back. I wish you'd stay."

"Sorry."

"Can I come with you?"

I shook my head. "I'll take you to a hotel and charge it to my client, under miscellaneous. What's Dick so anxious to talk to you about?"

"I wish I knew," she said helplessly.

Chapter 10

We had another drink while we waited for the water to boil. By the time we thought about food the water had almost boiled away. Shelley added more water, put in the spaghetti and broke out a fresh bottle of bourbon. The spaghetti, when we finally got around to it, was somewhat overcooked. Occasionally an eager youth just out of school will ask my advice about becoming a private detective. I always point out the hazards of the profession, among the most annoying of which are the irregular meals.

Shelley brought her coffee over to my side of the table. She was wearing the kimono I had heard about earlier. It was an attractive and practical garment, easy to put on and easy to take off, without any snaps or zippers to get out of order. She sat on my lap, which brought her within reach. I had already discovered that it was pleasant to reach for Shelley, but it was also time-consuming, and I kept a firm hold on my coffee cup. "Just saying goodbye," she said.

The kimono parted as she leaned forward, and after a time I realized that I was no longer holding the coffee cup.

"Is this what you call saying goodbye?" I said. "I call it more like saying hello."

"No, I know I can't make you stay," she said. "But I

want you to know you have my good wishes, and if you can spare any time later I'll be happy to see you. I'll get dressed." She added, "If you let go."

"It's a question of balance," I said. "These stools. I have to hold onto something or I'll fall over backward."

She laughed and got up off my lap. During the brief interval, my coffee had gotten cold. That is another trouble with being a private detective—things are constantly coming up so you have to drink cold coffee. I went to the bathroom to wash off the lipstick, feeling that I was on something of a treadmill. Then I reheated the coffee and drank it, made another cup and drank that, checked my .38, looked at the prints on the walls, and finally Shelley came out of her bedroom carrying her suitcase. She had put on fresh lipstick, and didn't offer to transfer any of it to me.

Downstairs, the doorman gave me a big salute, inclining forward at an angle of thirty degrees. "Yes, sir. That was—yes, the Buick."

I told him it was, feeling ashamed of owning a car that hadn't crossed water. He told me where I could find it and I paid him two dollars for the keys. After I drove off he maneuvered the cars on both sides of the gap so no stranger could get in. I took Shelley to the St. Albans. "Will you call me, Ben?" she said anxiously after she said goodbye.

"I'll see how things go."

"Give me enough for a double room. In case."

I gave her fifteen dollars. She whispered something to me. I didn't get all of it. I watched her walk into the hotel with her small suitcase, then I drove west to one of the one-way avenues, turned uptown and left the Buick in a garage in the 90's. I used the garage phone to call Mrs. Rooney, but Elmer hadn't reported in. Then I looked for the Riverside Drive address Davidson had given me.

It was a rent-controlled apartment house with two doctors' offices on the ground floor. I found Moran in the ladder of names in the vestibule, beside the number 7-E. The inner door was locked, but it was an elementary spring lock of the kind that is meant to reassure tenants rather than discourage thieves. I was working a strip of celluloid into the crack above the latch when I heard an elevator whir inside the building. I pulled the celluloid out and put it away.

I was rocking on my heels and studying the directory, hands in my hip pockets, when the door opened from inside and a man came out. I glanced at him casually. He gave me the classic double-take. We knew each other. His name was Chad Burns. He had a walk-up office off Times Square, and the legend on his unwashed front window read: C. BURNS, PRIVATE INVESTIGATION, WE INVESTIGATE HUSBANDS, WIVES, LOVERS; CHECKS CASHED. He was no relation to the more celebrated Burns Agency, and in fact Burns was probably not the name he had inherited from his parents. He was a large, sloppy man in his forties, who had investigated so many wives, husbands and lovers that he had lost his illusions, but he didn't investigate enough of them to make it possible for him to buy a new suit every year.

"Ben," he said softly, in a spurious Southern accent

which he had adopted for some reason of his own. "Ambulance-chasing, I see. This is not like you, friend."

"What ambulance are we talking about, Chad?" I said, holding the door.

"I study the papers," he said. "I have a good supply of reading time in the middle of the day, and I keep up with what the frat-brothers are doing. And what I learned today is that from now on you're going to be pecking for crumbs."

"I won't give you much competition, Chad," I said. "I don't have the right location for cashing checks."

He clawed at his face, as though he had walked into a cobweb. After he had finished overdoing his reaction he said, "I happen to be serious, believe it or not. If you got a first on something, would I walk in and cut your throat for a few measly dollars? No. I'd use the brains the good Lord gave me. I'd know that if I made a pest of myself I could mess it up for the both of us. I've been walking around a few more seasons than you, Ben, and I *know*. This time I got here first, so stay out of my hair, please, what there is of it. Buy you a brew?"

"Another time," I said. "I'm working."

He made an elaborate signal for secrecy, and took me into the inner lobby. "I don't blame you, Ben. You're new to the field. I flatter myself I'm a realist, and here's what I'm going to do. If you make out, I'll cut it down the middle. Fifty-fifty. I have the experience, you have the flash. Is that generous, or is it generous?"

"I don't want to hurt your feelings, Chad, but how would I explain it to my friends?"

"Let's not get too dichty with me, man. I've been

talking to people, and what people are saying is that you've lost some of those easy retainers. I'm not gloating, mind." He held up both hands. "I sympathize, because I've been through it myself. But a little realism, Ben. Use a little realism and you'll come out of this with flags flying."

"I'll bear it in mind."

"Do that." He thrust his face toward me, screwing his eyes into a ferocious squint. "But for some strange reason I don't think you mean it, so I'd better lay the whole deck on the table. I have connections with a certain amount of muscle. Disappoint me on this and we'll be watching for you."

"Always a pleasure to see you, Chad. Of course you realize I don't mean that either."

I walked away. He called after me, "Be realistic, Ben! Be human!"

I took the elevator to the seventh floor, found the Moran apartment and rang. Almost before I took my thumb off the button the door was opened by a girl in a shapeless wrapper. Her dark hair was pinned against her skull with plastic curlers.

"How many times do I have to—"

"I'm on the second shift," I said. "My name is Gates. Chad was probably up here shaking a tin cup, but all I want is information."

"Ben Gates?" She looked at me closely. "You don't look like your picture."

"That goes for a lot of people," I said. "Where did you see my picture?"

"The *Journal-American*, and you looked pretty frowzy.

Now that I've met you, it's been nice, goodbye."

She started to close the door, but I pushed against it and walked past. "Go on with what you were doing. I won't take up much time."

"Well, goddam me," she said. "Make yourself at home. I'm not going to talk to you. Why do I have to?"

"You don't have to," I said. "But you have to listen while I give you the spiel. Of course you can call the cops, but I don't think you want to go to the trouble."

"You're oh so right," she said. "I've had about all the fuzz I can take for one day. They picked me up at work and took me out to identify Leo. Go on with what I was doing. Sure. I was about to get in the tub."

"Well?"

She gave a short laugh through her nose. With the light on her face I saw that she was probably not much past twenty. In the curlers she looked like a juvenile edition of the Statue of Liberty, with everything from the neck down concealed in a heavy fog. But from the little I knew about Leo Moran, I didn't think he would be sharing an apartment with anyone whose proportions were less than adequate.

"Oh, hell," she said. "Sit down. You know that was the first stiff I ever saw? I threw up afterward, and they were all delighted. Lieutenant Minturn. There's a cat. You probably ran into him."

"He ran into me. What are you, the next of kin?"

"Well," she said, "I'm sort of his daughter. I'm not *actually* his daughter, but don't wear yourself out thinking about it, O.K.? My first name's Lorraine."

"How do you do?"

"I can do without the sarcasm, thanks." She picked up a watch from a table. "Sweet Jesus!" she exclaimed. "I've just got time for a fast rinse. There's gin in the kitchen if you want a drink, but watch the mess you make. I don't have time to clean up."

She disappeared into the bathroom with a rustle of the long skirt. I looked around the living room, which was very neat. Several overlapping copies of *Fortune* lay on a low table in front of the sofa. Even with curlers in her hair, Lorraine didn't look like the kind of girl who habitually reads *Fortune,* but it is easy to be wrong about such things. I went into the bedroom. This was a one-bedroom apartment, the kind that is advertised by New York rental agents as having four and a half rooms. On one of the twin beds a black dinner dress was waiting. It didn't look like much without a girl inside it. I checked the bureau drawers, working fast and trying to make as little noise as possible. I could hear the roaring of the shower in the bathroom. The cops had only wanted an identification, and they wouldn't have bothered to search the apartment. Apparently Lorraine hadn't let Chad in, so I was first on the ground. I wanted something that would connect Moran with someone on my list. I was beginning to get an impression of the man, and it didn't seem to me that he was the type who would keep his secrets in a safe-deposit box. He would put them under his clean shirts in a bureau drawer.

I found the shirts. There was nothing beneath them. The shower was turned off as I started on the closet. At first I thought there was nothing inside but women's clothes. I found the men's suits inside a bulky and opaque garment bag. There were four suits and two sports jackets, all with the label of a well-known Broadway store, whose customers have one thing in common—they, too, are not *Fortune* readers. I was about to pull the zipper and back out when I saw several overloaded manila envelopes in the bottom of the bag.

"Gates!" the girl called.

I zipped the bag and covered the distance to the bedroom door in three strides.

"Yeah?"

"Do you see my drink?" she said through the crack in the bathroom door. "A martini."

"Sure, do you want it?"

I went back to the bedroom window, which led to the fire escape. It was locked, with the lower sash attached to the frame by two anti-burglar worm-screws. I loosened the screws and freed the catch, then looked for her drink.

I found it in the kitchen, beside a bottle of gin and a pitcher of melting ice. I poured off the water, added gin, swished it around and filled the glass.

I took it to the bathroom. "I beefed it up a little."

Her arm came out and groped in the air. I put the glass in her hand.

"Thank you," she said. "I'm going to need a little boost to get through tonight." She made a sputtering sound. "That's practically pure gin. Well, hell. They can't shoot me for trying. How would you like to make yourself a little bread?"

When I didn't answer she yelled, "Can you hear me?"

"I hear you, all right. Doing what?"

"That's the point. I'd have to map it all out for you, and do I have time? That Burns ghoul put me way behind. Bring your drink over to the door."

I took out a cigar and lit it. I could hear her moving around on the other side of the door, and there were several mysterious clinks.

"Do I feel like going out tonight?" Lorraine said. "I don't, to tell you the truth. But how do I get out of it? I'm not supposed to call the boyfriend at the office. I could leave a message at the Yale Club, but what if I said I had a headache or the curse or something? I'd have to get it signed by a notary public before he believed me. He's about ninety-nine years old, and the poor dear is afraid he has a rival."

Suddenly she threw open the door. "Are you smoking a cigar?"

She had a tiny blackened brush in one hand, but so far mascara was all she had on. I had been right about Moran's taste in girls. It had been very good. Undressed, Lorraine would never remind anybody of the famous statue on Bedloe's Island. Her breasts were still trembling from the violent way she had opened the door. She had removed the curlers, and her black hair fell almost to her shoulders.

"You *are*," she said accusingly. "No, no, no. Kill it this minute. It's important."

She realized, possibly from my expression, that she was somewhat underdressed. "Excuse me."

She stepped back, putting the door between us again.

"I don't object," I said.

"Never mind. The cigar. It's little things like that you have to think about. You'd be surprised how long cigar smoke stays in a room. If he smells a cigar in here, there goes your old ball game."

I stubbed out the cigar in an ashtray. Her next words were slightly distorted, as though she was putting on lipstick as she talked. "You're no tourist, Gates. You must be beginning to get the idea."

"Let me guess," I said. "You're getting dressed to go hunting for badger."

"Sure. And the trouble is"—her face and a slice of naked shoulder appeared in the doorway—"tonight was supposed to be the night!"

"What a time for Moran to get himself shot."

"Stealing somebody's goddam jewels!" she said indignantly, gesturing with an eye-dropper. "Does it make sense? But it's like Leo, in a way. Always looking for something new."

"You didn't know about it?"

"If I'd known about it I would have locked him in the closet." She went back to the mirror. "But don't ask me any questions yet. First let me tell you what *I* want."

"I know what you want. You want me to come in after he takes off his pants, and tell him how much it's going to cost him. Chad Burns is your man."

She made a negative sound. "I know *something*

about human nature. Give Chad a handle, and the first thing I know he'll be using it on me. And would he be believable? These things you have to consider."

"He's older than I am," I said.

"Well, for you," she said, "I was thinking you might be my brother. I just got out of parochial school. To show how much they trust me, my family let me have my own apartment. But I'm very, very square. Nobody ever told me where babies came from. Leo made me a birth certificate that says I'm sixteen. The boyfriend is married, and he won't want anybody to know he's been caught in the sack with a sixteen-year-old. Seventeen or eighteen, he could claim I solicited him. That's what Leo said, and he ought to know."

"How old are you really?"

"Older," she said briefly. "You make gruesome martinis, did anybody ever tell you?"

When her face was finished, she came out of the bathroom clutching the wrapper. For the short trip to the bedroom, she didn't bother to put it on.

"I'm meeting him for drinks," she said. "I'll have a glass or two of dry sherry, and because I'm not accustomed to alcohol it'll make me sleepy. So instead of going out for dinner, I'll invite him up for spaghetti."

"For what?" I said.

"Spaghetti. It's the one thing I know how to cook. I really doubt if he'll say no. He's been asking to see my little apartment so he can buy me a house-warming present. One more glass of sherry up here and I'm helpless. He'll have to put me to bed. After the light goes out, give me a half hour. Aren't you even a little bit interested?"

As a matter of fact, I thought I was looking at her with considerable interest.

She said impatiently, "In the deal, in the deal!" She started for the bedroom, and the half-turn brought her into profile. The wrapper concealed her from only one angle. She gave me a swift look through the blackened eyelashes.

"Of course we might work out something later," she said. "I mean, it stands to reason. Not that I think you're likely to fall apart just because you see a girl without any clothes on."

"I still have control of myself," I said. "Barely."

"Then I'd better get dressed, because I'm saving it for Mr. Right. Come in the bedroom with me so I don't have to shout."

On the way to the bedroom I glanced at the door to the hall. It had a double-lock, with the kind of bolt that can only be cut with a torch. I stopped in the bedroom doorway. She had dropped the wrapper. She lifted her hands above her head and stretched. I believe this is known as the hard sell.

"That's right," she said as I smiled at her kindly. "My motives are obvious. I want you to think of the future. Your mouth is now supposed to be watering. Is it?"

"I'm drowning, Lorraine," I said.

She lowered her arms. "Fine. Now how does twenty-five percent sound? Leo did the masterminding, and I'll be doing all the hard work. I won't give you an overall figure, but his Dun and Bradstreet rating is double-A. Leo thought it might be milked for fifty thou. And no risk, that I can positively guarantee."

I didn't say anything, and she said quickly, "Don't say yes or no right now. Leave it open. I'll give you the keys and you can think about it."

I looked more receptive at the mention of keys. I wanted to look in those manila envelopes in Moran's garment bag, without having to chop through the wall.

"If that's how you want to do it," I said reluctantly. "But I can tell you now that the answer's going to be no."

"I'll take a chance. If this is a moral position you're taking, I'll really have to introduce you to my admirer. He's the creepiest." She stepped into a small fragile garment, smoothing it over her hips. "He's leaving all his dead-presidents to Yale when he dies, which is any day now, in my opinion. I mean, you aren't robbing anybody. Yale's so rich they won't miss it."

Stockings were next. After they were securely anchored she put on her shoes. "So think about it, will you?"

She gave me one final look across the bed, took a deep breath in case my attention had been wandering, and picked up the black dress.

"To put me in the right mood," I said, "did you ever know a guy named Pattberg?"

She looked as though a new smell had entered the room. "Slightly." She shook out the dress and pulled it over her arms. "He dropped in one night, and when he saw me he wanted to know if I'd ever thought of going into pictures. Leo laughed like hell and they went out for a drink."

She lifted the dress carefully, taking pains not to damage her makeup.

"That was the only time you saw him?" I said when her head emerged.

"That's all. He got killed the next day. I think Leo used to do business with him, before my time. What's the connection?"

"That's what I'm trying to find out. Leo didn't have anything to do with supplying the movies Pattberg showed that night?"

"I doubt it. I could be wrong. Before today I would have sworn Leo had too high an I.Q. to go robbing in the country. I need help with this zipper."

"How about a girl named Anna DeLong?"

"Who's she?"

"Or Dick Pope—Richardson Pope, Jr. Did Leo know him?"

"The zipper, Ben."

I found the tag of the zipper somewhere along the lower reaches of her spine. I ran it up, not without difficulty. With anything on underneath, the teeth wouldn't have meshed.

"There," I said. "Don't take any more deep breaths."

She ran a brush through her hair in front of the mirror. "How do I look?"

"Not much like a girl who just graduated from parochial school."

"Oh, I don't have to pretend with *you*." She looked

at me hard in the mirror. "I've been doing this wrong.
You don't care about that twenty-five percent, do you?
You don't care about—" She gestured at herself with
the hairbrush. "You want people to love you so they'll
let you watch their wedding presents again. You're a
goddamned tourist after all. All right, you cooperate
with me, I'll cooperate with you. I can tell you lots
of interesting things about Leo Moran. But not now.
Afterward."

She threw down the hairbrush. "We're going to
need a picture for insurance, in case he gives us any
trouble." From a shelf in the closet she took a small
Japanese camera with a flashbulb attachment. "Leo
worked out the stops for just the right amount of light,
so leave everything alone. It's loaded with infrared.
You know how to work these?"

"They're not too complicated. I have one like it."

"Come in quietly, exactly half an hour after the
light goes out. I'll see that he's busy. Say 'Lorraine?'
and shoot from the doorway. I'll have him lined
up. Then turn on the light and we'll ad lib it from
there. Don't blow your stack or anything, because we
don't want to give him a heart attack. You're shocked.
You can't understand it. Stammer. I'll get him out fast
and we can squeeze him later. Leo never even mentioned money till the second interview. Here's the
keys. If you decide not to do it, put them in the
mailbox."

"Maybe I'll come and see you some night when I'm
not busy," I said. "How long have you and Moran been
working together?"

"It couldn't have been long, could it, Coach, considering that I'm just sixteen?"

She put the camera carefully on a chair next to the door. She looked around. "How did that window get unlocked?"

She clicked back to the window, locked it and tightened the side screws. Returning to the living room, she picked my cigar out of the ashtray and gave it to me to put in my pocket. She rinsed out her martini glass and put away the gin. Then she turned on the exhaust in the window air-conditioner to air out the room. She left one lamp on.

"That's the one I'll turn off," she said looking around nervously for the last time. "It's the third from the left seven floors up. God, I wish Leo hadn't been so stupid. You go out first, Ben, and *think*."

Chapter 11

I didn't have to do much thinking. After taking the elevator to the lobby I walked up to the second floor and watched the lights. The elevator went back to seven and brought Lorraine down. I rang, rode the elevator upstairs, and used the keys she had given me.

Turning on the ceiling light in the bedroom, I took the bulky envelopes out of the garment bag and laid them on the floor. Moran had run a systematic business. There were half a dozen folders, each containing the relevant material for a single case—letters, canceled checks, IOU's, newspaper clippings, photostats, a tearsheet from one of the defunct scandal magazines, occasionally a photograph. I turned the pages rapidly, looking for a name or a face I would recognize. In the fourth folder, I found it.

It was a glossy five-by-seven photograph of a bed with two people in it, a man and a woman in the standard divorce-court pose. They had been unpleasantly awakened by a private detective with a camera. The man, tousled and scowling, was beginning a threatening gesture. The woman at his side had raised herself on her elbows and the sheet had slipped, exposing most of one breast. Her expression was oddly relaxed as she looked at the camera, all but smiling. I wasn't really surprised to see that it was Anna DeLong.

She was younger but easily recognizable. There was nothing in the folder but the single picture. I turned it over; there was nothing on the back.

I looked at my watch, but before I had time to see what it said I heard a key being slipped into a lock.

I snapped off the light. I had to move fast. Apparently something had gone wrong with Lorraine's plans, and she was back early. I shuffled the folders together, keeping out the one with Anna's picture in it.

There was a sudden stamping in the other room, an exclamation, a small scuffle.

"Obliged," a man's voice said. "I was wondering how I'd get in. Nice of you to remember old Chad."

I went on stuffing folders into the envelopes, hoping I could get out the window before anybody looked in the bedroom. I stopped abruptly. It wasn't Lorraine who answered.

"Let go of me," Anna's voice said. "Let—go of me."

"Stay loose, daughter," Burns said easily. "I'm not about to harm you."

I waited an instant, thinking fast. The little Japanese camera was where Lorraine had left it, loaded for bear.

Anna must have come for the picture, and I decided that the thing to do was to let her find it. Picking up the camera, I screwed down the focus, aimed it at the picture and opened the shutter. I rewound the film rapidly and removed the cartridge.

The struggle in the living room continued. The coffee table with its neat array of *Fortunes* tipped over and Anna cried out.

I returned the envelopes to the garment bag and

unscrewed the clamps that held the window. A moment later I was on the fire escape. I left the sash up several inches from the bottom. The fight seemed to be over.

Burns said, "Aw—put it away, baby. That could go off and injure somebody."

"It won't be me," Anna said. "You're the one it's pointed at."

"What's got into you all of a sudden?" Chad complained. "I'm only trying to push a few bucks."

"Stand still and be quiet. I have to think."

For a moment I heard nothing. Then Chad said, "You used to be with Leo, didn't you? You look different in cheaters, but I recognized you the minute you came down the street. We both of us know that old Leo had some nice things going, and the minute you took out that baby .25 I said to myself, why not offer this lovely little lady—"

"I said be quiet."

"How can I be quiet? I've got to talk you out of pulling that trigger."

I raised the window a few more inches. I recognized the note in his voice. He was about to jump her. He'd been a little drunk when I saw him, and he'd probably had a few drinks since. He wouldn't be impressed by a girl holding a .25.

He continued. "That Leo was a smart onion. He wouldn't leave a set of directions, so any old slob could walk in and start taking. But you knew his methods. You can kind of sort things out. You don't want to be in the limelight. Tell me who to collect from and I'll do it."

"I only want one item," Anna said after a pause. "You can have everything else."

"Now I call that a fine offer," Burns said heartily, "and I'll take it. Some folks might think you happen to know there's only the one item that's worth squeezing. But what's the use of being on this earth if you can't trust your fellow creatures? What kind of item?"

"It's personal," Anna said.

"And you're the one he was squeezing? That must have been pure delight for Leo. I wouldn't care if I did a little squeezing like that myself."

He chuckled. He was still chuckling when he grabbed her. I saw them in the bedroom doorway as I slid through the window. He was trying to shake the gun out of her hand. She kicked at his legs. For an instant, as her arm swung around, the gun was aimed directly at me. I ducked, and Anna saw me. She jerked her arm hard, turning Chad so his back was to the doorway.

He swore and swung at her. Coming up behind him, I caught his arm in the crook of my elbow and twisted, bringing him around to meet a hard upward left to the side of the jaw. It was a good punch, and it caught him with everything hanging. For a fraction of a second both his feet were off the floor. He went backward and fell over the coffee table. The copies of *Fortune* cushioned his fall. I went after him, ready to nail him again if he tried to get up.

He had wrenched Anna's automatic out of her hand as he fell. I saw it on the rug. He was staring at me stupidly. I kicked at the automatic and he rolled and batted it away from my foot. He got it before I could get my own gun. We were both in motion. There was only one way he could stop me, and he fired to my left, a little high but low enough to make me realize that the next shot would be on the target.

I stopped with my hand inside my coat. He was panting, his shoulders against the sofa.

"You surprised me, Ben. Where were you, on the fire escape? All this interest—it goes to prove my point. There's money here."

"I don't suppose you want to divide it in three?"

"I don't even want to divide it in two unless I have to. Just spread your arms out to the sides. All the way. If I'm going to have any peace of mind I'll have to take that gun you were diving for."

I opened my arms but backed away a step. In the bedroom, Anna was going through bureau drawers.

"I don't like other people to handle my gun," I said. "It's one of the things I'm eccentric about."

"And how would you feel about being gut-shot with a .25?"

"I wouldn't like it," I said. "But wouldn't that be pretty drastic for someone who's working on spec?"

"On spec, Ben? I admit I was prospecting when I came to call, but now I'm getting more hopeful, I really am."

I went on backing until I could see into the bedroom without turning away from Burns. Anna was checking the closet.

"Before you shoot me," I said, "you might listen for a minute. Then we can put the guns away and talk percentages."

He came to his feet, the automatic almost hidden in his big hand.

"Move it along, Ben. Maybe somebody reported that little bang."

"We're both outsiders here. Lorraine and Leo have been working on something, and she seems to think it may pay off in big bills. She needs a stand-in for Leo. She made me an offer. What do you think? Should we move in?"

He relaxed, not in the way be was standing but around the eyes. "That's right open-minded of you, Ben. I still want that pea-shooter."

It didn't take Anna long to find the picture. As she came out of the bedroom, Chad stepped forward and pushed the automatic against my stomach.

"Don't be shy with me, Ben. This won't hurt."

I said to Anna, "What did you find, somebody's picture?"

Burns's face twisted, but he didn't look around. He reached inside my coat and fumbled with the .38, which was held by the spring clips in the holster. Anna passed him, going to the door of the bathroom.

"If that's my gun he's holding on you," she said coolly, "don't worry about it, Ben. There was only one bullet in it and he used that."

"Don't believe her, Chad," I said.

The twitch convulsed one entire side of his face. He glanced away from me to Anna.

"What have you got there?"

"Nothing that would interest you," she said.

"Let me see that!"

Anna went into the bathroom, locking the door. For an instant Chad was pulled in too many directions. He made a move to follow her. Bringing my arms together, I clapped both hands over his ears, and then chopped at his wrist. He dropped the automatic. I knew from the look on his face that there were noises inside his head. I took out my .38, and because I didn't want any more trouble from Chad, I slapped him with it. He sighed and pitched forward.

Stepping around him, I tried the bathroom door. Inside, I heard a rush of water.

I picked up the .25 and released the clip, knowing even before it fell into my hand that it was fully loaded. Anna came out of the bathroom without the picture, which had just been confided to the New York sewer system. I ejected the live round from the chamber and snapped it into the clip.

"It was loaded, after all," she said. "I'm dreadfully sorry. He might have shot you."

"I don't think so," I said. "Chad never shot anybody. That was for your benefit, so you'd realize you were dealing with a hard man. Are you ready to go?"

She looked down at Burns, who lay perfectly still, his toes turned in. "Is he alive?"

"He's breathing. You and I are going to carry him downstairs. That won't be easy."

"Why not just leave him?"

"We're in the same business. Besides, I kind of

like him. How much of him do you think you can carry?"

"About one-tenth," she said.

That left quite a bit for me. I flopped him over. He was breathing harshly, and the smell of bar whiskey was very strong. I hoisted him to a sitting position. Putting forth a tremendous effort, I raised him to his feet and threw one of his arms over my shoulders. Anna came in under the other and we managed to get him halfway to the door.

"Maybe we'd better drag him," she gasped.

I shifted my grip. He was beginning to sag. Without the help of a block and tackle all I could do was see to it that he landed on the sofa. He was still bouncing when the door opened and Lorraine came in. She was giggling, having just been goosed by her escort.

"Don't!" she shrieked. "Please don't! No, don't!"

Chapter 12

What she saw in her living room cured her of the giggles. She took a quick breath and gave a highly convincing scream which raised the short hairs on the back of my neck.

It seemed to have the same effect on the man she was with. Lorraine had prepared me for a randy old goat in his second adolescence. She had exaggerated. There are many Hollywood actors his age still playing romantic leads. He wore horn-rimmed glasses, and there were downward lines at the corners of his mouth, as though he might be secretly miserable, but that was the only mark his face showed of thought or trouble. You see similar faces every day on the business pages, uncandid portraits of second vice-presidents who have just been promoted to first vice-president. He had a huge bottle of champagne under his arm. The cad had been planning to get that little sixteen-year-old girl drunk.

"What—" Lorraine said helplessly. "Who—"

"Police officers," I said. "There's been a robbery. Don't be alarmed. I'd be very much surprised if anything was taken." I looked at the man. "Is this your apartment?"

He cleared his throat so violently that he nearly

blew off his glasses. "Well—no, actually. The young lady—"

I turned to Lorraine. "Your neighbor here saw a man on the fire escape. She called the precinct and luckily we were only a block away. He sapped my partner. I don't want to wait for an ambulance so I'm taking him in. You'll probably have some detectives before I get back."

I tugged Burns forward so I could try getting him up on my back in what is known as the fireman's carry, although it would take two normal-sized firemen to carry Burns. The little pull brought him back to his senses.

"Gates!" he yelled, and drove one of his fists into my face.

It landed on my nose, where even a feeble blow can be painful. I was out of balance, and I went back on my hands. He yelled something and came down at me. Anna caught him from above, delaying him enough so I could grab his arms.

"Chad!" I said. "It's me."

"I know damn well it's you! You—"

"You're going to be just fine, Chad," I said, shaking him. "Nothing but a whack on the head."

He finally gathered that something had happened while he was unconscious. Looking up, he saw Lorraine and her victim, who was clutching the doorknob. The wayward muscles jumped in Chad's cheek.

"Now do you remember?" I said. "He swung a sap at you when you opened the door. I had my hands on him but he got away."

Groaning, he closed his eyes. I helped him up.

"I'll take him to St. Clare's," I told Lorraine. "When the detectives get here tell them I'll be right back." As we passed the man with the champagne I gave him a hard look. "Don't leave until we get your name and address."

Anna came with us. I thought Chad was putting more weight on me than was necessary. When the door closed behind us Anna said in a low voice, "We'd better get out of the way or we'll be trampled. That man isn't giving anybody his name and address."

Chad laughed. I put him in the elevator and punched the button for the lobby.

"So that's what she has in the oven," Chad said excitedly. "Here's how we work it, Ben."

I pressed the red emergency button and the elevator jolted to a stop between the fifth and the fourth floors. "He won't wait for the elevator," I said. "He'll walk down. Let's give him a couple of minutes."

"Ben!" Chad cried. "Use the old noodle. What the situation calls for, it calls for a tail. He's going to rush right home to mama. We find out where he lives and start cranking out hundred-dollar bills. We can still say we're cops. We don't cut the doll in at all. Right?"

He pressed the lobby button.

"Wrong," I said, hitting the emergency button again.

"I don't get you, Ben!" He tried to pull me from the control panel. "You only have to smell the guy. He smells of tailor-made suits and cars and Miami Beach."

I took out my .38 and let him pull me all the way

around. The .38 clunked against the side of his head. He subsided gently.

"I thought you said you liked him," Anna said.

"I said I *kind* of liked him." I put my gun away. "How long would it take a man in a hurry to get down seven flights of stairs? About three minutes?"

"Make it four. I wouldn't say he gets much exercise." She laughed. "The poor girl is going to be furious. What did you think of that dress? You probably liked it, but I know that kind of figure. She'll start getting chubby in a year or so. Too bad."

She was excited and jumpy, and kept rubbing the tips of her middle fingers against her thumbs, not quite snapping them.

"Ben—have we been through enough together so I can call you Ben?"

"I think so."

"Let me get my thank-you's out of the way. You were a very welcome sight, climbing in from that fire escape. I don't think you can know how glad I was to see you. But how in heaven's name did it happen? What were you doing out there?"

"You know the answer to that. I had to find out which of my little menagerie had a connection with Moran."

"I see. And now I suppose you'd like an explanation from me?"

"Make it a good one."

She prodded the inside of her cheek with her tongue. "I'll have to be hazy on some of the details. I knew Leo years and years ago, when I was too young to have much sense. You may have gathered that he was an attractive man. I was fascinated and flattered, and before it was over I was a little scared. Leo liked to hedge his bets, and after I broke with him I knew he kept a photograph as a souvenir. I won't say any more about it except that I wouldn't want anybody to see it who knows me now. It's been hanging over me like that sword in the story. I found out he'd still been living in the old place. I had a set of keys, which I never dared to use when he was alive. I asked some questions in the neighborhood and found out that he'd been living with a girl, which didn't surprise me. I waited till she went out. Chad Burns saw me and followed me in."

She stopped. I said, "That's not all?"

"Isn't it enough?"

"Not nearly enough," I said. "What kind of jobs did you do for Leo—the same that Lorraine's doing now?"

By this time she was less excited. She took off her glasses, polished them on a handkerchief and put them back on, putting on at the same time the personality I had seen her wearing at the Popes'.

"I can't stop you from drawing your own conclusions, Mr. Gates."

"Ben," I said.

"Ben, then. But I didn't say I did any jobs for Leo. I'd be foolish to admit anything."

"When did you see him last?"

"Not for years. And that's really all I can tell you. Aren't those three minutes about up?"

"Four. How about the slug in my coffee last night?"

"I don't want to talk about that. If you were a real policeman, here's where I'd yell for a lawyer. Don't you see? One question would lead to another. I couldn't be sure what I'd be letting myself in for."

I held my thumb over the lobby button. "You're under no legal compulsion to talk to me. You can spit in my eye and all I can do is wipe it off."

"I have no intention of spitting in your eye. Try to understand, Ben. I had such a wonderful feeling of release when that picture went down the drain! I've suffered enough. I don't feel any neurotic desire to be punished for anything I may have done for Leo. All I want to do is forget it. Maybe people like you won't let me, but I'm not going out of my way to spread it around."

I pressed the button and we started down. "I'll have to tell Mr. Pope what I've found out so far—"

"I'll deny some of it. I may be able to explain the rest. I think he trusts me."

"How about Dick?"

"I don't know about Dick. I hope you won't tell him, and I don't think you're the kind of person who would do it out of spite. Anyway, I can't let you threaten me. It's not as though you have any proof."

"I saw the picture," I said as the elevator stopped. "Does that make a difference?"

I hadn't expected much of a reaction, but to my surprise it nearly knocked her down. Her mouth opened and her face was suddenly as blank as a wall. She put out a hand to steady herself.

"How—"

"I got there ten minutes before you and Burns."
She went on staring at me and I added, "It was in one
of the folders at the bottom of the garment bag. But I
didn't need to see a picture of you in bed with a mark
to know that you and Leo were working the badger
game."

She swallowed, and some of her confidence began
to come back. "There's a difference between guessing
and knowing. I didn't want anybody to see that picture,
ever. The expression on my face! I've had nightmares
about it. I was so high on reefers that I didn't know
what I was doing, and certainly I didn't care. But from
the picture you'd think I was congratulating myself on
my cleverness. Leo knew what *he* was doing when he
kept it." She checked her hairpins. "You really rocked
me for a minute. Why didn't you take it?"

"I wanted to find out how badly you wanted it."

"Well, you found out, didn't you? God, that was
close. If you and Chad hadn't been arguing I might
have been stuck with it."

I leaned down to get Chad's shoulders. "You don't
think you owe me anything?"

"No," she said. "That's the way it worked out."

I dragged Chad halfway across the lobby and stopped
to rest.

"But I didn't leave it entirely to chance," I said. "I
wanted you to find the picture, but I couldn't be sure
I wouldn't need it. So I photographed it."

"No, you didn't," she said coldly. "You're only saying
that to scare me."

"It's true that I'm trying to scare you, but I've got

the film in my pocket. You must have seen the camera in the bedroom. Didn't you notice the infrared filter? When Lorraine gave me her keys she tried to persuade me to come in and surprise them, and she wanted me to get a picture first."

"Maybe it didn't turn out."

"There's always a chance," I said. "But I don't have to get a really sharp negative, just one we can read. It was a good camera. Leo wouldn't economize on something that important. And I've got your gun, so you can't shoot me. You may have to be nice to me after all."

"You're as bad as anybody!" she said furiously. "That's blackmail."

"Sure it is. That's how district attorneys get most of their convictions."

I dragged Chad to the outer lobby and propped him beneath the mailboxes. Anna's face was working.

"Go over to the bar across the street and call St. Clare's," I told her. "Ask for Emergency. Give them this address and tell them a man's lying on the sidewalk. I'll clip him again if he starts to come out of it."

She didn't move until I looked up. "Go ahead, Anna. I want to be sure there's no fracture."

"You smug—conceited—horrible—"

She turned abruptly and started across the street. A man and woman came into the vestibule. They looked at Burns.

"Drunk," I said. "I've called the cops."

The man was in such a hurry to get out his key that he dropped it. After they had gone inside I waited. Burns showed no signs of intelligence and few signs of life. I saw Anna come out of the bar. By the time she was back I heard the siren. I pulled Burns onto the sidewalk and we walked away.

We stopped in a doorway and waited till the ambulance attendants had made the pick-up. Burns still took no interest in anything that was being done to him.

"Well," Anna said.

"Let's get a drink."

"Ben, I know you'll think I'm being difficult but I can't help it. If you actually have that picture I know I have to tell you. Then it's up to you. But wouldn't I feel foolish if the picture turned out to be no good?"

"It might be a big weight off your mind if you told somebody."

"Oh, no. This is one weight I want to keep on my mind."

"I can rig up a darkroom at my place and we can find out for sure."

"That's what I was getting at," she said. "And then, if worst comes to worst—" She took my arm. "I never know where I am with you, Ben. I don't know if you're for or against."

"Neither do I," I said. "Has Dick Pope asked you to marry him?"

She didn't answer. Apparently I couldn't expect any rewarding conversation until I found out if I had succeeded in capturing her picture on the 35-mm film. The garage man found my Buick and we drove downtown in silence. Anna was far over on her side of the front seat, no doubt figuring the odds. I figured a few of my own and, after I found a parking place, took Anna to my apartment and showed her where I kept the liquor, I called Mrs. Rooney.

The phone rang five times before she answered. "Finally," she said. "I dozed off on the sofa. Now I can put in for overtime."

"You can put in for it," I said, "but unless somebody pays me you may not get it. Did you hear from Elmer?"

"I did, and I've got his time schedule if you want it, but what it all boils down to is not such a hell of a lot. Mr. Pope, Jr., got into a white Mercury in front of such-and-such an address on Central Park West. Drove up to the country so fast he nearly gave Elmer combat fatigue. Made a phone call—outdoor booth. Met somebody by the side of a highway, and this is what you're going to want or I'm a lousy guesser."

"Less editorializing, Mrs. Rooney," I said.

"Are you in a hurry?"

"Excuse me. Take your time."

"This was on a curvy road up near I think he said Prosper. I made a good note of it some place, don't worry. No street lights up there, so he had to ditch his car and work back through the forest. By that time there was another car behind the Merc. A black Pontiac. Elmer got the license and he'll call the Bureau in the morning unless you want to. He couldn't tell if the driver was male or female. He lost the tail there because he couldn't get back to his own car in time. But he went to where the guy lived, and the white Mercury was in the garage. He's been calling every half hour to find out what you want him to do."

"I'm home now. Tell him to call me here. If you've got a pencil and paper I want you to write something down."

Anna came in with the drinks as Mrs. Rooney said, "All right."

"A girl's name, Anna DeLong." I spelled it for her. "I asked her up for a nightcap, and I don't know much about her except that she carries a gun."

"That's D-e-capital L? O.K., Mr. Gates. If you're found dead in the morning, I'll tell the cops. Any address?"

"She lives in White Plains." I looked at Anna, and she gave me a street address which I repeated to Mrs. Rooney. "Another thing. She used to shack up with Leo Moran. Put that down, too."

"Le-o Mo-ran," Mrs. Rooney said. "I suppose she's lovely. That's the thing about your work, as I was saying to Mr. Rooney half an hour ago. It's chancey. People think they're entitled to take a shot at you any time they feel like it. You put in a lot of overtime you don't get paid for. But you do meet some attractive girls."

"Unattractive girls don't get in so much trouble," I said. "Good night, Mrs. Rooney."

Anna gave me one of the drinks as I hung up. "Very clever. I think I'm actually beginning to like you, Ben. God knows why."

I set the drink down without tasting it. "I'll see how your picture turned out first. Maybe you can find something on television. I'll be with you in half an hour."

"Half an hour, Ben! I'd be dead in ten minutes. Let me watch. I'll be good."

I didn't think she meant it, just as I wasn't sure that she hadn't put rat poison in my drink along with the ice and whiskey. Still, it was a challenge. Could I handle a 115-pound girl in a darkroom, or couldn't I?

"O.K.," I said.

It was a one-man bathroom. I told her where to sit and advised her to sit still. I locked the door from the inside so she wouldn't be tempted to throw it open at a crucial time and fog the film. After I took the developing tank and the chemicals out of a cupboard I turned off the light and loosened the bulb.

"Spooky," she said in the darkness. "Surely we don't have to wait half an hour to see if we have a good negative?"

"We'll know that in ten minutes. But you can't tell much from a thirty-five negative. You'll want to see how it prints."

"Speak for yourself, Ben. I don't want to see—" The end of the magazine came off and I removed the tightly-rolled film. Anna must have been wound up just as tightly. In the single vulnerable second when the film was out of the magazine and not yet in the tank, her hand darted forward and a lighter flared. I swung away, clapping the film into the tank with my hand over the opening. There was a spatter of breaking glass. I clubbed at the lighter with the tank until she dropped it. It went out as it hit the floor, and we were again in darkness. I felt among the broken glass on the shelf until I found the cover for the tank. After I screwed it on I tightened the light bulb and turned on the light to see how much damage she had done.

She had broken a bottle and knocked the hypo beaker off the shelf. That was all right. I had replacements.

"This stuff splashed all over me," she said. "What is it?"

"Sodium hyposulphite. Has it started to burn yet?"

"No! Does it?"

"It eats through shoe leather," I said, exaggerating. "You can rinse it off in the kitchen."

"I'm really soaked," she said.

We both stooped for the lighter. I got there first. It was a handsome piece of machinery in an alligator case, with a small silver plate engraved with the initials R. P.

"Junior or Senior?" I said.

"Junior, I think," she said, taking it out of my hand. "He's always leaving things around."

I let her out of the bathroom and locked the door. I measured the developer and poured it into the tank. While it was working I cleaned up the broken glass, giving the tank an occasional shake. I smoked a cigar and thought about my problems. I came to only one conclusion, as a result of which I took Anna's .25 apart and removed the hammer spring. I assembled the gun again and put it back in my pocket.

When enough time had passed I changed the solution. I was using a rapid mixture, and four minutes later I was able to take out the film to see what I had.

Thirty-one negatives were blank. The thirty-second looked a little overexposed, but I could compensate in the printing.

I unlocked the door, leaving the negative under the cold-water tap.

"Too bad," I said. "It won't win any prizes, but it's—"

I stopped. Anna had taken the pins out of her hair. She was sitting on the sofa wearing one of my shirts. The sleeves were rolled up above her elbows, the collar was open. Sonia Petrofsky had given it to me on my last birthday, a faint red and black check. It was a good shirt. It wasn't exactly transparent, but it wasn't exactly not transparent, either.

"That sodium whatever it was got on everything," she said.

"On everything?"

"Everything," she repeated firmly.

"Are you sure you're comfortable? Got everything you need?"

"I'm fine. What's the matter with you?"

"Not much air in this bathroom. Well, relax. Take off your glasses."

I retreated, locking the door again. I shouldn't have been that surprised. Like Lorraine, she had been Leo Moran's girl.

I set up the enlarger and worked for a while under a dim red light. Then I called her. I rocked the printing paper gently in the tray, watching the figures begin to form, the anonymous victim, gesturing angrily at the camera, the smiling girl beside him. They seemed to float effortlessly up from the depths where they had been hiding. Anna probably couldn't see them too well, having followed my advice and taken off her glasses. After glancing at the picture, she watched me.

"Where do we start?" I said. "With the coffee?"

Chapter 13

After fixing the print I hung it from the shower curtain to dry. I gave her some wire hangers, and she hung up her wet clothes. Each time she reached upward for the shower curtain, the shirt-tail climbed in a way that helped to take my mind off my troubles.

I locked the negative in my filing cabinet, poured the drink she had made for me into the sink and made another.

"You're a cautious bastard," she said, "What do you think I am, a registered pharmacist?"

"I just don't want you to get in any more jams. You're in enough already. Was that all you could find to put on?"

"What's the matter with it?"

"I didn't say there was anything the *matter* with it. But I have some pajamas. They'd be too big for you too, but at least they have bottoms. Or how about my raincoat?"

"Ben, you know you don't want me to bundle up in a raincoat. Don't be silly."

"It's just that I've been interviewing girls since six o'clock," I said. "Very different types, but they all seemed to think there was only one way to win my friendship. I mention no names. After a certain point I need to rest."

She was laughing, her hands on her hips and those red and black checks moving in and out. "Do you think I deliberately splashed acid on myself so I'd have to take off my clothes? But you've got something I want, and since I *did* splash acid on myself I'd be stupid to put on a raincoat instead of a good-looking, comfortable, roomy shirt. And when girls make these advances to you, don't you tell yourself that it's a good way to find out what they want you to do?"

"Not only that," I said gloomily. "I enjoy it."

"Come and sit down. I'll tell you about the coffee."

She sat on the sofa. There was room beside her, but I sat in a leather sling-chair designed to hold only one person at a time. I wanted a certain amount of fresh air between me and this girl.

"I'm half-blind without my glasses," she said. "So any time you want to come over on the sofa where I can watch your reactions— I know. The coffee."

And drugging the coffee, after all, had been simple. There were three coffee pots in the pantry. Anna had hidden two. She broke open several sleeping capsules she stole from her employer, pouring the powder into the remaining pot. When she told Hilda Faltermeier to take coffee to the gentleman in the library, the cook had made up a powerful mixture by pouring coffee on top of the barbiturates she hadn't known were there. Later, when Davidson and Minturn had been busy, Anna had washed the pot and the cup and saucer and put them away.

"Are you going to admit this to anybody but me?" I said.

"I hope I won't have to. The next question they'll ask me will start with why. But if I have to choose between that and having you put the picture into circulation, I'll admit I was working with Leo on the robbery. Not because he made me but because I wanted the money. Would that help?"

"A little."

She rapped her fist against one bare knee. "*God!* When Leo showed up out of the blue, after all those years, if I'd only gone to Mr. Pope and told him the whole story! Well, I didn't, and now I'd better start thinking about how to stay out of jail."

"Let's go back. What made you leave Leo in the first place?"

"Throw me a cigarette, Ben."

There was a pack on an end table near me. I shook one out for her and she lit it with Dick's lighter. I went back to my leather chair, which creaked in protest as I sat down. Anna breathed out a mouthful of smoke.

"What you meant," she said, "was why that girl in the picture left Leo. But the picture's wrong, Ben. I wasn't that girl even then. And even if I was, people change! Before I met Leo, I was one of the most conventional girls in the state of Michigan. I had a perfectly nice respectable set of middle-class parents. I had two sisters and a brother who are all married now and members in good standing of their local PTA. That sounds nasty. They actually are quite nice, but I don't see them very often. What happened to me to get me in that picture instead of the PTA? Leo Moran happened to me. He was an act of God, like polio. I got over him, the way most people get over polio now, but I was pretty paralyzed for a while, from the moral sense down. It only happened twice, that scene in the picture. I didn't mind it the first time, but the second time cured me. As far as Leo Moran was concerned, my temperature was back to ninety-eight point four. I moved out without even taking a toothbrush. I got a typing job with Mr. Pope's company. But I was always worrying. Sooner or later I knew Leo would find me. So when Mr. Pope was looking for someone to work for him out of town, I asked for the job and got it."

"Were you and Leo married?"

"He needed the wedding certificate—you can get in trouble without one. We had a justice-of-the-peace wedding in Maryland, but I always thought it might not be legal. He had a wife before me, and I doubt if he got divorced."

"When he caught up to you, it was through Pattberg?"

"How did you know that? Yes, Pattberg saw me the day he came out to reconnoiter. He wanted to be sure there was a back way out in case of a raid, I guess. I didn't think he recognized me. He only saw me for the tiniest part of a second, and he never knew me well. But creatures like that have a special instinct for things they can turn into money. And do you know how much Leo paid him? Five dollars. That's how good Leo was. Leo let a few weeks go by before he showed up in White Plains. By then I'd almost stopped worrying. He had the picture with him, in case I'd forgotten. He wanted a percentage of my salary, and I wouldn't have been taking much home every week, after taxes and after Leo Moran. I might as well tell you—Dick came to my apartment quite late one night when Leo was there. They didn't run into each other, but Leo saw Dick's car outside and traced the license number. This made things more serious, because if there was one person I didn't want to see that picture, it was Dick."

"How do you stand with him at the moment?"

She drank before replying. "It can go either way. He's finally broken his engagement to the Hardwick bitch, which is a giant step. I'd better be frank with you, because sometime before tomorrow morning I want to ask for some advice. I want to marry that boy. I don't feel the same way about him that I did when I started with Leo, but once like that may be enough for one lifetime. I think I'd like him just as much even if he wasn't so rich. Maybe not. It's mixed together, and you wouldn't believe it anyway. But I'd be good for him. I'll just add one thing. Needless to say, I haven't discussed this with his father, but I'm pretty sure I have his blessing."

"Who had the idea for the robbery? You?"

"You're so flattering. Yes, it was my idea. I had to do something in a hurry. Leo would never have done it just for Mrs. Pope's jewels or just for the wedding presents. Both together he couldn't resist. I knew him fairly well. He was a little shamefaced about the way he made his money because there was so little real danger. If it didn't work sometimes, it just didn't work—nobody ever wanted to take it to the police. The robbery would be dangerous, but not too dangerous. He insisted on wearing a gun to make it romantic, but what appealed to him most was the touch about drugging the detective who was watching the wedding presents."

"Everybody liked that touch but me," I said. "How were you going to split?"

"You don't understand. I wasn't going to take any money. Not that I have any objections to money, but I couldn't risk it. The deal was that he'd go to Nevada and divorce me, getting *that* out of the way, and he promised to destroy the picture. I knew he wouldn't, but if he ever tried to use it I could turn him in for robbing the wedding. I recorded one of our conversations at my apartment. The recording canceled the picture, you see? It was a stand-off. Can I make myself another drink?"

"I'll get it," I said. "You disturb me too much when you walk around in that damn shirt. I've finally got my mind on this, and that's where I want to keep it.— Don't lean over," I said as she reached for her glass. "Sit perfectly still."

I made her the new drink and brought it back. "How much did Leo expect to clear?"

"A hundred thousand," she said, taking the glass. "And I had to get a photostat of the insurance before he'd believe me. I confess I blew it up a little."

"Did he have an outlet lined up?"

"I didn't ask him. He knew all kinds of people."

"What I'm getting at—and I'd appreciate it if you'd fold your arms for a few minutes—is whether you told him there was money in the safe."

She did what I'd told her—she sat still.

"There wasn't, was there?"

"Let's do it the way they teach the rookies at the Police Academy. One of the rules is not to let the suspect ask you questions."

"Am I a suspect?"

"You're suspect number one, and if you want to put on that raincoat now I'll hand it to you."

"All the more reason not to put on a raincoat. What am I suspected of doing?"

"Of stealing seventy-five thousand dollars. This isn't academic with me—I get ten percent of anything I recover. I doubt if you could get Leo interested in jewelry. It's hard to get rid of. Cash is something he understood."

She drank. "You're right, Ben, and I wish I'd thought of it—it would have saved me a good deal of argument. But I didn't. Who— Sorry. I almost asked a question."

"I'll answer that one. Who told me about the money in the safe? Mr. Pope."

She gave a good impression of a girl who was thinking hard. "Do you think he could have been lying?"

"It's possible. Maybe he wanted to give me an incentive. He told me a couple of other things which turned out not to be true. Did you set up an alibi for the time Leo was in action?"

"I couldn't, Ben. He had to stay in the dressing room until Mrs. Pope unlocked the safe. We didn't know when that would be. I tried to be in the kitchen as much as possible, but I didn't think it was important."

"So you might have been walking guard outside the door while he tied her up. When he came out he might have given you some of his parcels to carry."

"Why would he give me seventy-five thousand dollars?" she cried. "*Leo?* Leo Moran didn't hand people packages of money unless he had a very good reason. And I wasn't outside Mrs. Pope's bedroom. I didn't know there was money in the safe. And if Leo took it," she added, "what's happened to it?"

"Are you sure you don't know?"

"Damn sure."

"What we could do," I suggested, "is play that recording you made of your talk with Leo. If the money wasn't mentioned then, I'll believe you."

"Yes, we could do that," she said bitterly. "You know I erased it a couple of hours ago. That's the first thing I did when I got home."

"Well, the theory was that if I could find Leo's inside connection, I'd find the money. Maybe it's not that simple. I'll talk to my client about some of the untruths he's been telling me, and see where we go from there."

"What will you tell him about—" She made a sweeping gesture.

"I don't see why I shouldn't pass on most of it," I said. "Of course if you want to change your mind about having the money, we might be able to fake up a story that would please everybody."

"Then I wish I had it. But I don't, and seventy-five thousand dollars is more than I can raise." She picked up her drink and gave me a brief look. "But we don't have to decide anything right this minute. Let's sleep on it."

I let that lie for a moment. Hilda, Shelley and Lorraine were all fine upstanding girls, but they didn't compare with Anna. In addition, she was present while the others were scattered over two counties. In addition to that, she was more nearly my age.

"Yes, it's getting late," I said. "I don't suppose your clothes are dry?"

"Oh, I don't think I'd want to go all the way to White Plains. The trains get very gloomy this late at night. I could go to a hotel."

"In wet clothes? No, you'd better stay here, so long as you realize that there's another thing they teach the rookies. You aren't supposed to spend the night with a suspect. Sometimes you can't help yourself, as the authorities realize, and if it happens you're not supposed to let it influence you."

She finished the drink in one long swallow and came over to me, more and more luminous inside the shirt. "Then it's settled?"

She leaned down and kissed me. Before long she was in the chair with me; somehow we made room. While she kissed me she fooled with the back of my neck, the way girls do.

She drew back and said seriously, "Do you think I didn't mean it when I said I'm in love with Dick? I meant it." She kissed me warmly. "He's dumb and innocent and wild, and I don't know what will happen to him if I don't marry him. At the same time, you're quite—well, quite—"

I wanted to say that it was a shame I didn't have a few million dollars to go with it, but she was kissing me again. When I had a chance I said, "Let's do it the way they teach the rookies. Let's move some place where we have room to maneuver. I haven't had my clothes off for two days, which I can't say for the people I've been associating with. Ten minutes. I'll take a shower. I'll shave."

She rubbed her fingers the wrong way across my jaw. "I like it like this."

"I'll put on after-shaving lotion."

"You smell very nice as you are, Ben." This was getting ridiculous. Finally she let me get up and go into the bedroom. I came back in a robe. I checked myself halfway to the bathroom and returned for the key to the filing cabinet.

"Don't you ever forget you're a detective?" she said.

"Give me time."

In the bathroom I took down the picture and slid her clothes along the pole so the shower curtain would close. I turned on the water. A moment after I got under the shower Anna opened the door and called, "How do you turn on the record player?"

I told her. As soon as she left the bathroom I got out of the shower, dripping, and listened. One of my Gillespie records came down onto the turntable. Dizzy raised his horn and began to sound reveille, making enough racket so I wouldn't hear anything else, such as the opening and shutting of the outside door. I gave it another minute, wrapped a towel around me, and went out. Anna was gone. So was my beat-up raincoat.

So, I found on checking my pockets, were the keys to my Buick and the .25 automatic. That seemed to cover everything. She already had the lighter.

The phone rang. I turned down the volume before I answered it.

It was Elmer, asking permission to sleep at a motel. Dick Pope was put away for the night. Lights were beginning to go off in the Pope house.

"I won't be surprised if he has one more errand," I said. "You know my Buick? He'll be meeting a girl driving one like it. I'd like to know what they say to each other, but that's probably too much to expect. After that never mind the Mercury. Stick to the Buick."

"O.K., Ben. How soon do you want to know?"

"In the morning. We all want to be fresh. The girl has an apartment in White Plains. When you check her in there you can knock off."

I put the phone back and turned up the music. Gillespie was in the middle of another long, demented, driving solo. I finished my drink and went back to finish my shower.

Chapter 14

I dreamed that I was caught inside a burning building, and I woke up with my heart sounding the rapid shallow beat of panic. A siren was wailing. After a moment I remembered that this was New York, where if you want to hear a siren all you have to do is listen, and I got out of bed and put on the water for coffee.

I was in the middle of my second cup when the phone rang. I took the coffee into the living room.

"Ben?" Elmer's voice said. "Good morning. I have some stuff for you."

I sat down, juggling the phone and the coffee cup. "Let's have it."

"I went back to the Popes' after I talked to you. Pretty soon a light went on upstairs. I had a good spot down the road, and I picked up the Mercury when it went by. He went to a tavern, the Three Deuces. There were only four or five cars there, and one of them was a Buick. Like your Buick, hell—it *was* your Buick. The boy had a package, and I took a couple of chances getting inside fast to see what it was, but it was just a pair of high-heeled shoes. A very nice-looking dish was waiting for him. Dark hair, glasses. She had a raincoat on that was too big for her, and she kept it on."

"No wonder," I said. "It was my raincoat, and all she had on underneath was one of my drip-dry shirts."

"*Now* you tell me," Elmer said. "They were in a corner booth. They did a lot of low talking, but the place was so empty I couldn't get near them. I went to the john, and he was holding a paper napkin to his face. Was he crying? I don't know, maybe. Then I thought I'd better get back outside, because this was out in the middle of nowhere, not much traffic. The girl left first. I picked her up O.K. She took a couple of screwy turns, and ended up in one of those roadside places, a turn-out with a couple of picnic tables. There was a car already there, a Pontiac, and it was the same Pontiac our boy's Mercury conferred with earlier. Interesting?"

"Did you see who was driving?"

"No, I had to go past, and she was only there a minute. This was bad country for a one-car tail, and I almost lost her. But I put her to bed in White Plains, finally. Do you want the address?"

"I've got it. Give me the Pontiac license."

"I've checked that, Ben. I know a guy in Motor Vehicles and he called it in for me. It's registered to Joseph Minturn. M-i-n—"

"Minturn!"

"Yeah, does that fit? A Prosper address."

"It wasn't a State Police car?"

"Not unless it was disguised. A three-year-old Pontiac, a bad scrape on one side."

"These things are going to start meaning something pretty soon. How much sleep did you get?"

"Less than usual. But I'm available."

"I'll send Irving out. I can use you both. When's the funeral?"

"One of the troopers said eleven."

"I'll tell Irving to bring you a dark suit. He'll fill you in."

"I've been reading about it in the papers, Ben. Very educational. They didn't have anything about a girl wearing nothing but Ben Gates's raincoat."

"Let's hope they don't, too. I've had too much of that kind of publicity."

I found Davidson at home and gave him instructions. I called the St. Albans, but Miss Hardwick, they told me, had checked out. No one was answering the phone at her Central Park West apartment. I tried Anna DeLong in White Plains; there was no answer there either. After that I put in a personal call to Mr. Pope in Prosper.

A maid tried to tell the operator he wasn't taking any calls, but I broke in.

"He'll talk to me. This is Ben Gates in New York."

In a moment I heard my client. "Gates?"

"Do you want to talk now or wait till later? You told me to report when I found out anything, and I've picked up a few things."

"Having to do with the money?"

"Not exactly. You've got too many extensions on that phone, Mr. Pope. I'll feel better if you can call me back from somewhere else."

"Is it important?"

"I think so."

He agreed reluctantly, and I gave him my number. I poured another cup of coffee while I waited.

The phone rang.

"Ben?" Shelley Hardwick said. "You stood me up. I waited and waited, and finally I put on my pajamas and went to sleep."

"I got involved. Where are you? I tried the hotel."

"I came back to the apartment to change. The phone was ringing when I came in—was that you? I thought if you're going to the funeral you might want to pick me up and we could go together."

"I may not get away that soon. Shelley, you've had all night to think about it. Have you any idea why Dick wanted to talk to you last night?"

"I didn't waste any time thinking about it. I gave up expecting any rational actions out of Dick long ago."

I told her I might see her later at the Popes' and said goodbye. The ring came an instant after I put back the phone.

"I'm in the gardener's cottage," Mr. Pope said. "It's a private line. What did you want to tell me?"

"Have you seen your secretary this morning?"

"Yes. Apparently you were rough with her last night."

"That's one of the things you're paying me for. Did she have any ideas on how to keep me from going to the District Attorney?"

"We don't think you'll do that so long as there's a possibility of collecting a seventy-five-hundred-dollar fee."

"Ouch," I said. "You know that she and Moran were married?"

"That's not entirely certain. In any case that issue died with Moran, and as far as I am concerned nothing is changed. I want to make my position clear. I understand that the weapon Moran used against her, to force her to do what she did, is now in your possession. I don't wish to know what it is. I realize that only something extremely incriminating could have made her help with the robbery. In her judgment you are not offering it for sale. Is that correct?"

"It's a photograph, Mr. Pope. Even if I wanted to sell it, she couldn't be sure she'd bought anything. I could make any number of prints before I turned it over."

"Which makes it difficult, doesn't it? She puts forward this suggestion. She is willing to be charged with being Moran's accomplice. Not his wife, his accomplice. The jewels have been recovered, the insurance company will have no reason to be vindictive. The judge, of course, will be informed of my wishes, and I would expect the charges to be dismissed. Your fee, in the full amount we agreed on, will be forthcoming at once. Today, if you like."

"I'm glad to see you think it's serious. Are you going to get a new secretary?"

"I haven't thought that through. I may have to."

"And will you make Anna pay you back the seventy-five thousand?"

"Gates, I—" He stopped.

"Or wasn't the subject mentioned?"

"I am liking your tone less and less. This would be between me and Miss DeLong. The police know nothing about it, so it wouldn't have to come out in the public announcement."

"The only person who seems to know about it is me, and I've had moments when I didn't think it was real. Isn't there a part of Anna's suggestion you haven't told me about? I've got two men working on this. Wouldn't I be expected to call them off and go out and get drunk?"

"I will contribute a case of Scotch," Pope said.

"I don't know, maybe it's the best we can do. I'd like to talk to you about it first."

"That's out of the question, I'm afraid. I've just had a rather sobering visit from my doctor. He has ordered a vacation, to start at once. I'm leaving for Maine directly after the funeral."

"Then I'd better come out right away."

"No, don't. I'm interpreting my medical advice rather broadly. I've had enough worry, enough trouble, enough excitement, and I am putting too much effort into keeping my voice down right now. Let me put it simply. I regret having given you any status in this, but at the time I thought it was necessary. I am now withdrawing that status. You can co-operate along the lines of Miss DeLong's suggestion, refurbishing your reputation and earning a rather high fee, or you can be foolish and come out of it with nothing at all. I will leave the check with Miss DeLong to handle as she sees fit. Before I leave I will give Lieutenant Minturn appropriate instructions. Is that clear?"

"It's not clear at all," I said. "She rushed you. Hold on for a minute. I haven't spent all the retainer yet, so in my dumb way I still consider you a client. Did Dick set the fire that burned down the recreation building?"

I listened to telephone noises for a moment. Finally he said, "That was looked into at the time. It was established that—"

"Who did the looking?" I said.

"The insurance people. The volunteer fire company. The State Police. I assure you that if there had been the least shred of evidence—"

"That kind of evidence is hard to find, Mr. Pope. That's one of the bad things about package insurance. If the package is big enough, there's a tendency to settle small claims without being too picky. I hear that Dick started going to a psychiatrist after the fire. Was it connected?"

"Not in that sense. There were disturbing things about the party besides the fact that it ended with a fire. If I'd been convinced that Dick deliberately started a fire in which someone was killed, I wouldn't have stopped at sending him to an analyst. I would have had him committed. Will you get to the point, please?"

"I have to ask about the money in the safe. You told me something about a tax case. That was easy to check. There's no tax case, although I ought to warn you that I stirred them up and they're going to take a look at your back returns. Was there some other reason you didn't want to tell the cops about the money, or wasn't there any money?"

"I see no reason to continue this," he said. "I mentioned a possible tax prosecution because it was something you could understand. At that time I wanted an investigation. I now have the answers to some of the questions that were bothering me, and I want the investigation to stop."

"You can always hang up on me, Mr. Pope."

After a moment, when he remained on the line, I said, "I hear Dick has been short of cash lately."

"Who told you that?" he said sharply.

"Nobody had to tell me. It's in the air. He used to drive a Ferrari, now he drives a Mercury. He's been borrowing money from people who don't have it to lend."

Pope said reluctantly, "The boy was idiotic enough to get into a dice game run by a professional gambler. The gambler now holds certain IOUs. I say it was idiotic. I don't say it was out of character."

"How much does it add up to?"

"Twenty thousand dollars. You're right, I should hang up. That's what Anna advised. Telling about it only makes it worse. That's why I kept money at home —I never knew what mad thing Dick would do next. Signing IOU's to a professional crook! There I drew the line. I told him he could expect no help from me. In the end I probably would have paid, I always do. But he had been threatened with a beating, and I thought if I let them give it to him perhaps it would teach him something. I won't appeal to your sympathy. I doubt if you have any. But he's my son! I've done what I could with him. I know it hasn't been enough. His mother—lived in her own world. When Dick was young I had no time." He said suddenly, "The hell with you, Gates. Go to hell. Go to hell."

And he slammed down the phone. I looked at the phone at my end, then got a dial tone and phoned Sonia Petrofsky to ask if I could come in and look at her morgue clippings.

"I've been expecting you," she said. "I'll leave them on my desk."

I phoned Grand Central to get a list of departures for White Plains. Few people wanted to travel in that direction at this time of day. If I missed the next train I would have to wait another hour. Nevertheless I finished my coffee and smoked a cigar before I moved. I took a taxi uptown, spent fifteen minutes in Sonia's office with the clippings, and caught the White Plains local after it had already begun to move. I had bought a morning paper, but I had enough on my mind without worrying about the bad news from other parts of the world. I looked out at the scenery, which wasn't impressive, and thought about all the people who had been lying to me for the last day and a half. In White Plains I gave Anna's address to a cab driver. My Buick was waiting in front of her apartment house. It was locked, but I had an extra key taped inside the fender below the gas hatch.

Twenty minutes later I was in Prosper. Before I talked to anybody I wanted to find out more about that fire.

The one-truck fire house was locked up all around. An old man who had nothing better to do watched me try the doors.

"Salesman?" he said.

"I'm looking for the chief," I said.

"He's more than likely down at the store."

He pointed to a hardware-fuel-and-feed store at the other end of the main street. It stood on a slight rise, like the castle of a baron who levies tribute on the surrounding country. In a sense this was fitting, for most of the furnaces around here burned oil. It had its own rail siding and storage tanks, an accretion of sheds and warehouses, and looked considerably more prosperous than the small bank across the street. I parked beside two school buses, went into the hardware section and asked a lady where I could find the fire chief.

"He had to go to a funeral, but he ought to be back any minute," she said. "Can I help you?"

I told her I'd wait. A hardware store that keeps up with new gadgets is a pleasant place to waste time on a summer morning, and before I had been there long I had bought a combination cork-puller, bottle-opener and can-opener, which could probably also be used for pulling teeth.

"There he is," the clerk said. Looking out the display window, I saw a heavyset man coming out of the bank. "I didn't think it would take long. He wasn't going to the cemetery."

The man crossed the street and came in, loosening his tie. He had short legs and a chest like one of his own kegs. He took off his dark coat, hung it on a wooden hanger and started rolling his sleeves.

"Did anybody take care of you?"

"I was waiting to see you," I said. "I want to ask you about a fire. My name is Ben Gates."

"Gates," he said. "I was reading about you. You mean the fire at the Popes'? What about it?"

"How did it start?"

He had stopped rolling up his sleeve when I told him who I was. Now he finished that sleeve and started on the other.

"We turned in a report on it. There's a copy at the fire house, anyway there ought to be. We had to certify it. What's your angle, Gates?"

"My angle?" I said politely.

"You know what I mean. The insurance had a man on it for a week or more. What was his name again?— Hamilton. I thought the thing was supposed to be closed."

"I'm working for Mr. Pope, not the insurance company."

"What's *he* want to rake it up for? You'd think he'd be the last—"

He looked around. The clerk had gone into an office and I could hear a typewriter working. He lowered his voice. "Because at the time there were these rumors around that the fire was of incendiary origin."

A man in jeans and an OD Shirt, with a hairline mustache and half-circles of coal dust on his lower eyelids, came in by a side door.

"Here's Al," the chief said. "He'll tell you the same. He was driving that night. They collected on the insurance, so why not leave it alone?"

"The man who was shot the other night used to be in business with the projectionist," I said. "Pattberg, the man who died in the fire. If there's any connection

Mr. Pope wants to know about it. You probably know the law on this better than I do. If somebody set that fire, couldn't he be slammed for manslaughter as well as for arson?"

"I've heard people argue it could be second-degree murder."

"So naturally you were pretty careful about what you said in your report."

"Damn right we were careful." He came out in front of the counter and parked one meaty hip. He felt for a cigarette. "People are going to gossip about a thing like this, it's human nature. And one of the things the Nosy Parkers have been saying is that we leaned over backward because Pope showers down to the party coffers every other year. After the fire he made the Volunteer Company a present of a two-way radio, which is where he made a tactical mistake in my opinion. It made the talk flare up all over again. What it all comes down to is this, and I've probably been through this rigamarole a couple of hundred times. We're firemen one night a week when we drill, and sometimes on Sundays when we take and wash the equipment. We march in the parades, and once in a blue moon we get an actual conflagration. Unless it's a chimney or brush or something on that order, usually all we can do is stand around and watch it burn. I manage a fuel and hardware business here. Al drives a coal truck for me. It's the insurance man you're going to depend on. He's the expert. It's to his company's financial advantage to prove the fire was set. And his report was unanimous. The fire began in the projection booth, more than likely from a dropped cigarette."

"Wasn't there a kind of explosion?"

"According to the eyewitnesses." Al, on a nearby counter, stirred and half-grinned. "Now it's a fact that the eyewitnesses were three-quarters or more looped, but you wouldn't think they could all be mistaken like that. And that's the way films would go up, with a boom."

"It was out of control by the time you got there?"

"Was it out of control! It was a still night, and those flames were shooting up a hundred feet straight in the air. What we did, we put out our fire lines and so on, and we damped down the roofs of the other buildings. And, as I say, we watched it burn."

"Not to mention that we watched the eyewitnesses," Al said.

"Yeah," the chief said, "that was quite some party the boys and girls had been having."

"How many other companies answered the alarm?" I said.

"We had two more before the night was over. But we saw right away there wasn't any use rousting a lot of hard-working people out of their beds."

"How many from your company made it?"

"Just about everybody, in due time. I beat the engine personally, and how many others would you say, Al? Three or four?"

"About."

"And when did Hamilton get there?"

"The following morning. As soon as the ashes were cool he stirred them around and made tests and I don't know what all. They have ways of telling."

The phone rang in the office. The clerk put her head out of the door.

"Your brother on the phone, Mr. Minturn. Want to call him back?"

Chapter 15

"No, I'll take it," the chief said.

As he went into the office another driver came in from outside. He was young and clean and red-haired, with the shy manner and nice smile of workingmen painted by Norman Rockwell.

"Rusty," Al said, smiling reminiscently. "Talking about the big fire. Rusty's wife belongs to the ladies' auxiliary," he explained. "When she showed up with the rest of the ladies to serve us hot coffee and doughnuts, naturally she looked all over for her husband. But no Rusty."

"I wish you guys would lay off," Rusty said. "I was around. Just because she didn't see me right away—"

Al chortled. "And were you lucky she *didn't* see you right away. A little hefty, that doll, but in the right places. I wouldn't complain about getting a piece of that myself."

"Goddam it, Al! Will you cut it out?"

"Minturn," I said thoughtfully. "Is his brother the state trooper?"

"Oh, yes," Al said. "Important man. Without him there's a question if New York State could get through the rest of the week."

"Which one drives the Pontiac?"

"That's the chief, why?"

"I just wondered. I guess I've got everything I need. Tell him I couldn't wait."

I started for the door. Minturn called from the office, "Gates!"

I tapped my watch, going through a pantomime of being late for an appointment, and kept going.

"Al!" the chief called. "Hang onto him."

Al swung off the counter and stepped into my path. His thumbs were hooked into his broad belt and he was smiling lazily, as though he couldn't stop thinking of the crazy wet-haired girls at Dick Pope's party.

"Hang onto me?" I said. "What's the matter with *him*?"

Minturn came out of the office. "My brother's in the troopers, Gates. When I mentioned I was talking to you he practically busted my eardrum. A few questions he wants to ask you. He's coming right in, and the way he sounded he'll really goose that Chevy. He's been known to make it from Popes' in seven minutes. Stick around."

"Tell him I'm sorry I missed him," I said. I tapped my watch again. "Sometimes there aren't enough hours in the day."

I started around a counter. Minturn cleared his throat. He must have signaled to Rusty, for the boy moved over in front of me.

"And what is this?" I said, stopping.

"A couple of questions, for God's sake," Minturn said. "You aren't that busy."

"Boys, boys," I said. "Go play with your fire engines."

Turning, I headed for Al. He took his thumbs out of

his belt. He had developed those shoulders swinging a big shovel, but the mustache on his upper lip made me think that he might not care to be cut up in somebody else's quarrel. I could have been right, but I never found out. Rusty stepped out of his *Saturday Evening Post* cover and clubbed me from behind.

The store was full of hard objects he could have used, but he didn't need to use anything except his fist. I went down on one knee. If there hadn't been a counter to hold onto, I would have gone all the way. I shook my head. It didn't fall off, so I pulled myself to my feet.

"That's the last time I buy any can-openers in *this* store," I said.

That, at least, was what I was trying to say, but the words bled into each other. Minturn said nervously, "What was that? Never mind, you're not hurt. Get a chair for him, Al. The lieutenant wants us to keep him here so he can bounce his ass over the town line himself."

I heard that over the sound of the road-building machinery inside my head. "I thought he just wanted to ask me some questions."

"Well, you know—I was being diplomatic. I don't want any trouble. A customer might walk in."

"This is the wrong way to go about avoiding trouble. What's your first name? Joe?"

"Yes."

"What I'm trying to figure out, Joe, and maybe you can tell me, is why would anybody go to the bank after coming back from a funeral? Why did you even think

you had to go to the funeral? You can't know the Popes
that well. You're not one of those people who like to
listen to sad music. Does your brother know about all
the driving around you did last night, all the people
you met out on the roads? Or is he getting a cut?"

I didn't expect an answer and I didn't get any. I was
killing time until things were back in focus.

Minturn's store was running a sale on house paint
that month, and a pyramid of gallon cans had been
erected in an open space where two aisles came together. As soon as I was able to read the fine print on
the labels I lurched away from the counter, staggered
as though I was still feeling Rusty's blow, and knocked
over the pyramid.

A customer came in from the street, a stout matron
in Bermuda shorts, carrying a dachshund. Rusty and
Al tried to kick aside the paint cans so they could get at
me. More cans came down. I picked up a double
handful of loose nuts and bolts and threw them at
Rusty, then whirled and went for Minturn.

He opened both arms, thinking only of blocking
me from the door. I dived at his midsection. My out-
stretched fingers went into his stomach like a fork into
a sausage. He went backward, and I hit him with a
display of small tools, a rack of hinges and a basketball
hoop. That was all I could reach.

I vaulted onto the counter and kicked at Al's head as
he came up the aisle. The customer screamed and lost
her dachshund, which leaped out of her arms and
darted forward, yipping sharply.

Minturn grabbed at my leg and my foot came down

on his hand. Rusty was still caught in the rolling cans. I took two rapid steps and went over the roll of wrapping paper at the end of the counter. Even without counting the customer and her low, excited dog, there were too many people in the store. I ran into a back room where bulkier objects were kept, things like garbage pails and trash burners. Coiled lengths of plastic garden hose hung from a long peg near the door. I grabbed the topmost coil. As Minturn charged through I dropped it over his head. I spun him around with a straightarm, bouncing him off the wall. While he was still vibrating I hit him with a left. I knew as it landed that I wouldn't have to bother about this branch of the Minturn family for a while.

I knocked over a stack of galvanized pails and made a tangle on top with wire and bamboo rakes. All this was helping relieve my nervous tension, but I knew that in a moment Al or Rusty would think of circling the building to get at me from the rear. The big double doors to the yard were open. I would have a clear run to my Buick.

At that moment Rusty ran around the front of the store. I ducked back.

I saw another door. In another moment I was in a covered gallery filled with sorted lumber. This brought me to a warehouse running parallel to the store. I pulled open a hanging door. Another door began to slide at the other end of the warehouse. I stepped back quickly and climbed a ladder to the second floor of the gallery, where there were long racks of moldings. Inside the warehouse on this level was the feed-loft, a kind of half-balcony. I climbed in through an open window.

Al was in the doorway below me, looking cautiously around. He was carrying a baseball bat. I checked the windows overlooking the yards. There were three. A truck loaded with pea-coal was parked beneath the third. I opened that window, listening to Al poking around among sacks of dry plaster and cement on the ground floor.

"Come out, come out, wherever you are," he called.

In the last minute or two things had been happening fast, but now I slowed down. I gauged the drop to the coal truck and decided I could make it. I waited till my breathing was more or less normal. I could hear Al working his way diagonally across the warehouse floor toward the steps to the left. I picked out a fifty-pound sack of grain and dragged it to the stair-opening, a simple rectangle cut into the loft floor. Al would have heard me if he hadn't been making so much noise of his own.

"Gatesy!" he called. "Where *are* you?"

His shadow fell on the stairs. I tipped the sack on end, holding it by its ears. When he put his foot on the bottom step I called urgently, *"Al!"* He stood still, looking around, and I let go.

I ran back to the window. Swinging out, I dropped onto the truck, going into coal to my knees and my elbows. I waded forward to the cab.

The key had been left in the ignition. When the motor took hold I cramped the wheels, reversed and came forward hard. The yard had only one exit, past the overhead oil tanks and along the railroad siding. I heard someone shouting. As the driveway straightened I could see the main street, and I began to think I was going to get at least that far. Then a Pontiac sedan made a skidding turn into the driveway and slowed to a halt fifteen feet in front of me.

I hit the brakes. Minturn—the fire chief Minturn— came out of the Pontiac looking a little shopworn. He had something even better than a baseball bat—a sixteen-gauge shotgun.

I stepped out onto the running board to look the situation over. Rusty and two other men appeared around the warehouse at a hard run. They slowed as they saw Minturn. He came forward, holding the shotgun at ready-arms. It looked as big as a 105 howitzer, as shotguns do in town. And then I noticed that it was brand new and I stopped worrying.

I took out my .38, snapping off the safety and forcing a round under the hammer. Rusty and the others stopped short. With two guns showing they seemed considerably less eager.

Minturn brought the shotgun around so I could look down the barrels. "Put that pistol on the fender and be quick about it, Gates. I don't want to do it, but if you make one move I'll blow you out of your shoes."

"Not with an empty shotgun," I said.

He sneered. "You want to take a chance on that, do you?"

"I think so." I walked to the front of the truck, holding the .38 beside my leg, pointing at the ground. "You grabbed that gun out of the case as you went by.

It's still got cosmoline on it. You're wasting time here, Joe. You ought to be over at the bank cleaning out your safe-deposit box. That money's hot. You'd better bury it."

"I warn you—" he said in a choked voice.

I really didn't think he'd had time to load the gun, but I would have felt foolish if he had proved I was wrong. I stopped beside the front bumper.

"How about you fellows?" I called to Rusty and the others. "Can you hear me? Joe's been blackmailing the Pope boy. He didn't share the loot, so you don't want to get a share of the fallout."

A car stopped in front of the warehouse. A door slammed and Lieutenant Minturn came up to the group. He pushed his hat back from his forehead and looked from his brother to me and back again.

"What have we here?" he said. "The gunfight at the O.K. Corral?"

"He didn't get away from me, by God," the chief said, lifting the shotgun. "And you can have him. You ought to see the store!"

"Well, Gates," Lieutenant Minturn said mildly. "Let's disarm. Joe, put that Browning back where you got it."

The chief aimed the gun at the coal pile and yanked one trigger. There was a loud bang and a small convulsion in the side of the pile.

"You know so much," he said.

I laughed and started to put my gun away, and suddenly the fire siren sounded.

Chapter 16

It was a high wail—a real fire and not a time-signal or a make-believe air-raid. For an instant we all stood still, as though we might have to pay a forfeit for moving.

Lieutenant Minturn was the first to get back into action. "What are you standing around for?" he asked his brother. "You're the chief."

His brother unfroze and ran off with the shotgun. Rusty and the others disappeared. I heard a car start.

Lieutenant Minturn came past the Pontiac. He raised his voice so I could hear him above the siren.

"Maybe I ought to be surprised, but I'm not. I figured you all along for a hard-nose."

"What's happened now? Did my client change his mind about me?"

"You no longer have a client, and that puts us back where we started. I was talking to Mr. Pope not more than half an hour ago. He said if you had the goddam effrontery to show up around here again, I was to take whatever action appealed to me. And that I will do with pleasure."

"I'll have to talk to him. I think I can change his mind again."

"You won't get the chance. He was leaving for the airport."

"Maybe I can catch him."

I started around him. "Gates," he said amiably, "I wouldn't do that if I were—"

And he threw the sucker punch, a right hook that was supposed to make me stand still for the combination. But I expected it, having noticed that he had taken out his upper plate. I slipped the punch and caught him by the wrist and under the armpit. Pivoting, I threw him in the direction he was already going. I might have broken my own record for distance, but the coal truck was in the way. Minturn slammed against it and slid slowly to the ground, leaving a dented radiator grille.

It took him a moment to remember where he had seen me. He groped for the front bumper, seeming to know that I wasn't going to help him. The siren warbled a few times, then returned to its sustained scream. Leaning over, I flipped back the front of his coat.

"Not carrying a gun," I said. "That makes it simpler. I'd just as soon not do any more fist-fighting today."

I took out the .38 again and moved it in front of his eyes. "You got here late. You didn't hear the loose charges I was throwing around. Your brother Joe collected some blackmail from Dick Pope this morning. A good guess at the figure would be twenty G's. He came back from the funeral and put it in the bank. I had a tail on Dick last night, and he met Joe out on the highway somewhere. And I doubt if Junior is the type who would go to jail rather than stool on a pal."

I dropped the gun in my side pocket. Minturn watched it till it was out of sight.

"Get up," I said. "All by yourself. I could put a slug in your knee and get away with it. You've been riding me for a couple of days, and people might wonder if that doesn't prove you're in this with Joe. But if you are, I don't think you've had time to get any of the dough. There's still time to cop out. I want to talk to Mr. Pope before he leaves. Let's go in your car and break the speed limit."

He dragged himself to his knees. Suddenly he made an anguished face, put his hand in his coat pocket and brought out the upper plate. The four important center teeth had been smashed when he banged against the truck. He made a little sound of dismay.

He began to recover only when we were out on the highway and he had built up his speed to over seventy. He flicked on his siren to pass another car, which gave him the illusion that he was again in charge.

"What did you say about blackmail?"

"That's right," I said approvingly. "Play it dumb. You remember the famous fire. Joe must have found something to show that the fire was set, something that would point the finger at Junior. Wouldn't a rich boy like Junior pay good money to keep out of jail? Sure he would, if he could raise it. He told his old man he wanted it to buy back some IOUs from a gambler. It didn't work. What Joe should have done was go to the father in the first place. This is all news to you, no doubt."

"So that's why—" Minturn said.

"You're doing fine," I said. "That's why nobody wanted to cooperate with Gates. Pattberg was buried. They wanted him to stay buried."

"I'll tell you this much," Minturn said with sincerity. "I investigated that fire, and believe me, if there'd been one single solitary thing to point to arson, brother or no brother—"

"You don't need to sell me, Lieutenant. You're safe as long as you act stupid. It's true that if that sneak-punch had landed back there, you would have gone on to beat hell out of me. But your motives were probably beyond reproach. You weren't trying to cover up for Joe for a slice of that twenty thousand. You were just running an errand for the big man on the grand list."

"I'm glad you realize that—"

He looked at me, his eyes narrowing. Then he looked back at the road. "Wait till I get my hands on that goddam Joe. I'll break him in two."

"Slow down through here," I said. "We might meet somebody on these curves."

He eased up on the gas and the needle dropped to 65. I heard more sirens shrieking ahead of us. We went into another curve, and as the road straightened out ahead I saw that the Popes' house was on fire.

"Holy Virginia!" Minturn burst out.

He pumped the brakes. One entire wing was ablaze, and I saw in a glance that this would be one of those fires where Chief Minturn and his volunteers could do nothing but stand and watch. Only one fire truck had arrived. A second was rocking down the highway toward us, a few firemen clinging to its sides.

Minturn let it go through the gate. We followed, eating its exhaust.

Minturn leaned forward over the wheel. "Do you think the son of a bitch started this one, too?"

"Why not? He got a lot of fun out of the last one."

People were running across the lawn. The cars had been brought around from the garages and parked on the grass away from the house. Irving Davidson was helping the Prosper firemen, who were unreeling hose. The lieutenant strode off to find something to do.

Now I heard the flames for the first time. It was like being close to the edge of a waterfall, and I no longer had any doubt that when the noise died down nothing would be left but the chimneys and a cellar hole. The wind was blowing hard, in the worst direction.

Minturn dispatched a trooper to the gate to keep out the buffs, but a scattering had already come through and were drifting about among the engines. I headed for another group of spectators, most of whom were still dressed for the funeral. Shelley Hardwick, in black and wearing a hat with a half-veil, ran toward me. Her eyes were alive with excitement. Being a detective, I deduced from this and a smell of gin that she had been drinking martinis in the dead woman's honor. "Ben—"

"Later," I said.

Dick Pope and Anna DeLong were off by themselves. Dick was hunched forward, one hand to his face. Anna looked over her shoulder as I came up. Her hairpins were all in place, and she was back in her role

of the indispensable secretary. It would have been
tactless to remind her that when I saw her last she had
been wearing one of my shirts.

"Where's your father, Dick?" I said.

He spun around. I had seen him in different moods,
but this was a new one. His eyes had an added surface,
like frosted glass, and behind them a fire was raging,
no less intense than the one that was burning down his
house. His face was as wrinkled as a very old man's.

He pulled away from Anna's arm and cried, "I
don't care!"

Whirling, he ran toward the engines.

"Ben, stop him," Anna said. "Don't let him—"

Dick veered and headed for the house, his head
down and his elbows churning. I made a disgusted
sound and set off after him, giving it everything I had.
I wasn't dressed for the hundred-yard dash and,
though he wasn't either, he had a start. He wanted to
get into that burning building, and I really didn't. Even
so, I gained on him. I felt a sudden wash of hot air. His
form was awkward and labored, his head going from
side to side as though he had just come into the
stadium after running the full twenty-six miles. In
another fifty yards I might have overhauled him, but it
couldn't be done in twenty.

"Dick!" I shouted, cupping my hands to my mouth.
"You meathead, come back!" I tried to think of something that would stop him. "Your father wants me to
tell you—"

It was too late. He ran up the front steps and into
the house. I retreated. Anna was running toward me.

"What did he forget?" I said when she reached me.

"He thinks Pattberg's in there! He said it was his fault, he had to save him. Ben, he'll be killed!"

"That's possible," I said. "Did his father get away?"

"Yes, Dick drove him to the airport from the cemetery."

Joe Minturn ran up. "If you think I'm going to send my boys in after him, you're crazy!"

"And if he doesn't come back," I said, "maybe you can keep that twenty thousand he gave you."

"Listen, if you think that has anything to do— Just try to get within ten feet of that front door."

I had my hands up to shield my face as I looked at the house. The stone front didn't seem affected by what was happening behind it, though masses of white smoke could be seen through the windows on the upper floors. The Prosper firemen were coming forward with a limp hose.

"Take off your skirt, Anna," I said.

Her fingers went to one hip. Then she looked at me. "What?"

"Let's have your skirt. Hurry up."

"If you're thinking about going in there," Minturn said, "you are *really* nuts."

I snapped my fingers impatiently, and Anna pulled the zipper and wriggled out of her skirt. I grabbed it. Minturn called after me, "Don't let the stonework fool you. The roof's about to fall in."

The pumper was working and the firemen had begun to get water. They played it on the roof of the long el, which was beginning to smoke. The man on the nozzle was Al, apparently undamaged after being hit on the head with a fifty-pound bag of feed.

"Look at Gatesy," he said when he saw me. "Lucky I've got my hands full or I'd take you over my knee."

I thrust Anna's skirt into the stream of water. "I'm going in. Wet me down when I get up close. Not yet! *Not yet!*" I shouted as he turned the hose on me.

I sprinted away, doing some broken-field running to keep out of the powerful stream. I hurdled the balustrade onto the terrace, then stood still and let the water hit me, turning until I was thoroughly soaked. I ran for the front door. There was a roar from the burning wing, an eruption of sparks. I wrapped Anna's wet skirt around my head and plunged in.

For the first second or two it seemed cooler, but as I ran toward the stairs the heat hit me again. Ragged streamers of smoke curled down the stairwell. I took a searing breath and ran up the stairs. At the top the smoke was too thick to see. Muffled in the wet skirt, I groped down the corridor, feeling along the inner wall for the door to Mrs. Pope's bedroom. I had to be right the first time. If I was wrong I didn't think there was anyone outside who felt strongly enough about it to come in to get me.

The roar from the burning wing seemed far away. I touched a closed door, and left it closed. The next would be Mr. Pope's. My lungs had to have air, and if there was no pure air available inside of three seconds, I would have to settle for smoke. Two-point-nine seconds later, my fingers reached a doorway. I burst through. I ran to the open window and butted out the screen. Leaning far out, I sucked air into my lungs.

Al aimed the water at me. In a moment I was being severely buffeted.

"Cut it—"

The stream caught me and knocked me sputtering back into the room. The air was better near the floor. For a moment I forgot what I was doing and tried to claw my way back to the window. Then I saw two figures lying near the foot of the bed.

I crawled across the room. One of the figures was Mr. Pope, who hadn't, after all, made it to the airport. He lay on his back, his head toward the window. Dick had been dragging him in that direction when he collapsed. I couldn't tell about Dick, but his father was still breathing. Pushing Dick off, I pulled at Mr. Pope and got him moving, keeping my head close to the floor. It was a clumsy way to pull, and when I was halfway I raised my head too high and got a lungful of smoke. I began coughing. Each cough was worse than the one before. For a moment I lay gasping, still gripping Mr. Pope's collar, and then the stream of water, wandering around the room, hit me and made me so mad that I came to my feet and dragged my client the rest of the way to the window. I put my head into the stream, waving both arms like a football referee signaling an off-side.

Davidson knocked the nozzle out of Al's hands. It leaped and slithered across the grass.

There was a *whoosh* behind me and a tongue of

flame licked in through the open door from the hall. It disappeared, but I knew it was still there, an ugly presence in the midst of the masses of smoke. New fire engines had arrived, and one, putting out a ladder, was trying to maneuver into position to reach me from the other side of the terrace. I couldn't wait. I yelled at Davidson. I reversed Pope's heavy body and wrestled him feet-first over the sill. Smoke was pouring out around me. The back of Pope's coat was burning. I slapped at the flames and put them out, and then lowered him slowly over the sill.

Davidson hadn't moved.

I yelled at him savagely. He couldn't have heard me, but he sprinted up the bank and rolled over the balustrade. To my surprise, Rusty was waiting below the window. I lowered Pope as far as I could, and let him drop into their arms.

I took a deep breath. A section of the plaster ceiling had fallen onto the bed. I dropped to my hands and knees and started to crawl toward Dick. His clothes were on fire. Smoke closed in and I could no longer see him. Another piece of ceiling came down. Fire broke through the floor between me and Dick. I still had Anna's skirt around my head, and when I realized that was on fire too, I decided the time had come to get the hell out of there.

I threw the skirt away and started to crawl back. The only part of the ceiling that was still where it should be, on the ceiling, was directly overhead. I couldn't see it through the smoke, but I knew it was there. It fell on me when I was still a foot or two from the window. Al reached in and grabbed me.

He pulled me out of the fragments of burning lath, and did a highly unprofessional job of dragging me down the ladder, bumping my head from rung to rung. When we reached the bottom two other firemen rescued me from Al and carried me out on the lawn. They laid me down with care, although it was a little late to start being careful. When I opened my eyes Al was grinning at me.

"As for the way you carry people down ladders—" I said.

"Gee," he said. "Nobody dropped a bag of chicken feed on you?"

Davidson came up. "I never thought I'd see the day when you turned out to be a hero, Ben."

"I always hate to lose a client."

"How about Junior?"

I didn't answer. I looked up at the burning building. The façade was still intact, but flames were visible through most of the windows, as though there was nothing but fire on the other side of the one solid wall.

I came to my feet. Davidson caught me. I saw an ambulance on the grass, with a little cluster of people near it.

"Is Pope over there?"

"They'll take care of him, Ben. You'd better take care of yourself."

"Do you think anybody has a drink they could spare?"

Al said, "Stop over at the engine. We carry a little medicinal whiskey."

I was badly in need of medicine. I started coughing again and had to sit down. By the time I got my breath Al was back with a pint of blended rye. I coughed the first mouthful back up but the next stayed down. I tipped the bottle and took several long medicinal gulps.

"Well, don't kill it," Al said. "You might not be the only one."

I poured some more medicine down my throat and waited for the explosion. When it came it lifted me to my feet and started me toward the ambulance.

"One thing you might want to know, Ben," Davidson said. "If you're still in business?"

I nodded.

"The boy's white Mercury. Elmer saw a guy take something out of the glove compartment. He took it back to his own car, which by a happy coincidence—"

"Was a Pontiac," I said. "He was picking up twenty grand of keep-quiet money. I know about it."

"Well, why didn't you say so?"

"Be kind to me, Irving," I said. "I'm in shock."

Anna was the only one I knew in the group around Pope. He lay on a stretcher while a young man in a white uniform tried to find his pulse. Anna's face was streaked and wet. Several strands of black hair had escaped, and her glasses were fogged. She gasped when she saw me, and threw herself against my chest. She said my name several times, as though to be sure she had the right man. I put my arms around her, as there is little else you can do with a girl in that position. I was surprised to see that she appeared to be crying real tears.

"They think he took sleeping tablets," she said. "He's been drugged. Why would he—"

At that moment Pope's eyes opened and he sat up, alarmed and angry. The only other time I had seen him his eyes had been concealed behind tinted glasses and his hair had been carefully brushed. If it hadn't been for the startled expression I still might have missed it, but as he pulled his wrist away from the intern, I realized that Pope was the man in bed beside Anna in Moran's picture.

Chapter 17

Feeling the difference in my arms, Anna drew back. She must have gone on hoping to the last. Even this final bit, coming in against me to cry on my pistol holster, had been to distract me until the ambulance could take him away.

My mind was racing, but because of recent events it was less of a sprint than a sack-race, a clumsy lurching from point to point. Moran hadn't been threatening to show the photograph to Anna's employer, who after all knew who was in it. He had threatened to show it to Dick, and it didn't seem probable that the boy would be ready to marry Anna after seeing her in bed with his father. And that was why she had been willing to go to such lengths to destroy it—not because the girl had her face, but because the man had Pope's. That was why Pope had been planning to leave after the funeral —they couldn't allow me to see him again.

Pope had covered his face with his hands. I had a chance now, but again I would have to be right the first time. The slug of raw whiskey on top of the smoke I had eaten was giving me a crazy exuberance.

I was still holding Anna lightly by the shoulders. "He needs some coffee," I told her. "The ladies are probably here by now. Get him some."

"Shouldn't he go to the hospital?" she asked, her

tone so flat and wooden that I looked at her sharply. She was rapidly coming unstuck.

"Not just yet," I said. "I'm the big hero, so they're going to let me talk to him first."

She turned obediently and walked off.

I took Davidson aside. "Somebody said something about a two-way radio. The Prosper fire chief is named Joe Minturn. Tell him to be a good dog and maybe I'll throw him a biscuit. There must be somebody around who can take shorthand. I want half the radio set-up over here, and at the other end I want the chief and his brother and somebody taking everything down. I also want that bottle of whiskey."

"I'd say you've had enough whiskey."

"I'll switch to brandy if they've got that."

As he started off I called, "Tell Elmer to find a girl named Shelley Hardwick and keep her on tap."

I returned to the ambulance. "All right, everybody," I snarled. "Move along, nothing to see here."

When I had everybody in motion but Pope and the intern I squatted beside the stretcher. Pope didn't seem to know me, and when I saw myself in a mirror later I understood why. Among other interesting effects, my eyebrows were gone.

"You know who I am, Mr. Pope," I said. "I'm the man you hired to find out what happened to the seventy-five thousand dollars."

He winced. "I'm—sorry about that."

"Don't be," I said. "I'm still hoping to collect that fee. I also pulled you out of the fire. Maybe you'll feel grateful enough to explain a few things."

The intern put in, "He shouldn't be doing any talking."

"It won't do him any harm," I said. "It may do him some good."

Pope blinked. There was a fluttering at the corner of one eye, and he covered it with his hand. "Anna says you saw the picture."

"Yeah. I didn't know it was you. I thought she was just embarrassed because she was naked."

Pope uncovered his eye and looked at the intern. "This is private."

The intern stood up. "You're sure it's all right?"

"Quite sure," Pope said heavily. The intern went to the front of the ambulance and Pope said, "I don't expect you to understand why, after that, I made her my secretary. It was the only time she—"

"She told me it happened twice."

"Once, twice, what does it matter? I made it clear to Moran that he could expect no easy money from me. And yet I didn't want to send them to prison. I was fond of Anna. As a secretary she has always been first-rate. When she said she wanted to break with Moran, I created this job for her. Of course," he added, "after the blackmail attempt our physical relationship didn't continue."

"Of course not," I said.

"I didn't suppose you would believe me."

A station wagon made a wide turn on the grass and pulled up beside us. The girl at the wheel was Hilda Faltermeier, the part-time maid who had brought me the coffee and sandwiches the night of the wedding. She was wearing a sweater and the tight, paint-spattered blue jeans I had already seen, and for some reason I was relieved to observe that there was more than one layer of clothing between Hilda and the outside world. She had a large coffee urn in the back of the station wagon.

"Are you in the ladies' auxiliary?" I asked.

She looked startled. "Sort of. You aren't—yes, you are! What did they do to you? You look horrible."

"I've been meaning to tell you your bike is checked at the railroad station."

"I was wondering." She studied me. "It's a shame, too. I thought your eyebrows were kind of cute."

I laughed, feeling better. "They'll grow back, if we have patience."

I turned down coffee and she drove off as Davidson drifted up on foot. He had a green metal box, about the size of a dispatch case, and he set it beside the rear wheel of the ambulance. He handed me the whiskey bottle.

"Hold on," the intern said. "He shouldn't have anything to drink."

I uncapped the bottle. "This is for me."

Pope looked around at Davidson. "Is this one of your men?"

"Mr. Davidson," I said. "He knows about most of this."

"The hell I do," Davidson said. "And I don't want to find out, either."

One of his arms was resting on the radio. By listening for it, I could hear the faint frying sound that meant the circuit was open.

"Guess what we've been talking about," I said to Anna.

"I know, I know. The picture."

The whiskey was hurrying through my veins on its way to the centers of thought and speech. I felt pleasantly relaxed, and for the moment I didn't dislike anybody. But there were several points in this father-son triangle still to be cleared up.

"How did you feel when Dick began getting interested in Anna?" I asked Pope. "It seems to me they used to milk this situation quite a bit in Greek tragedy."

"There was nothing tragic about it," Pope said. "Dick was in a very bad way. If we could have pulled it off it might have been the making of him."

I must have goggled at that. Pope insisted, "I mean it. Anna is a very competent person."

"Uh-huh," I said. "And what made you change your mind about taking the plane this morning?"

"Dick said he had something to give me. I thought it was the money. Minturn had orders not to let you in, so I decided it was safe to stop for a few minutes. I wanted Dick to get it off his chest. He insisted on making drinks. He must have put sleeping pills in mine."

His hand was trembling so badly that Anna took the coffee away from him and put it on the grass. She started to say something. I put my hand on her leg.

"You can listen," I said. "That's all I want you to do."

Pope rubbed his temples. "He was talking excitedly

about Anna. That's all I remember. He couldn't bring himself to give back the money—he was afraid of the beating he would get if he didn't pay the gamblers."

My hand tightened as Anna tried to speak. I was intent on Pope, but at the same time I was pleasantly aware that there was a leg under the nylon.

"Everybody thought we had gone to the airport," Pope said. "He—put me on the floor and started the fire. This time there can't be any question about it, I will have to send him away. I should have done it before."

"Did he know you were thinking of having him committed?"

"I'm sure he guessed."

"What makes you think he took the money?"

Pope blinked slowly. "Who else could have? He's the only one who knew it was there."

"You told him?"

"Yes, that night. I wanted him to realize that I could save him from the consequences of his folly, but I chose not to. He went in to say good night to his mother. She was dead, the safe was open. He had to find out if the money was gone. I understand that. It was just something he had to do."

"Tell Elmer we want that girl," I said to Davidson.

I was beginning to lose momentum, and I took another long drink. "I hope you made out a check for me this morning?"

"Anna has it. It's not payable. The agreement was that you would get it if and when."

Davidson came back with Shelley, who looked like a

schoolgirl who has been told to report to the principal's office.

"Hello, everybody," she said sullenly.

"Hello, Shelley," I said. "Tell these people who took Mr. Pope's seventy-five thousand dollars."

"I did," she said. "I didn't think you'd let me keep it."

"I suppose it's pretty well hidden?"

"I did my best, but you can probably find it."

"That's the wrong answer, Shelley. I'll put it another way. Mr. Pope doesn't want publicity because too many things would come out at a trial. So give us the money and I think he can be persuaded to forgive you."

"That's sensible," she said. "You realize, don't you, that you won't get the full amount?"

"We'll settle for fifty-five," I said. "I know where I can put my hands on the other twenty. How did Dick pry it out of you?"

"He cornered me on the phone this morning. He told me to choose. Either I gave him twenty thousand or he'd tell the police and I'd lose it all. So I chose."

"Hilda saw you in the corridor Saturday night in your kimono. What happened? You went to Dick's room to find out if he was sorry for some of the things he'd said?"

She nodded. "He wasn't."

"And then on the way back, one of the young delinquents chased you into Mrs. Pope's room?"

She went on nodding. "I don't know how it happened, Ben. I felt her. She was dead. I didn't think— I reached in and touched some envelopes in the back of the safe, and then I heard the shots. They scared me.

I didn't know I'd taken the envelopes until I was back in my own room, and I didn't look inside them until the next morning. Then I got drunk again fast, so I wouldn't talk myself into turning it in. I needed that money. I'm in hock to more people."

"How did Dick know you had it?"

"He figured it out, I guess. He remembered I left his room a minute or so before he heard the shots downstairs. And I'm an amateur. I suppose I acted guilty."

"All right, Shelley," I said. "Dismissed."

"He used the twenty thousand to pay his gambling debts?" Pope said as she walked away.

"He didn't have any gambling debts."

I held the whiskey to the light. Pope said suddenly, "I want a drink."

He put out his hand. When he did that he was used to having something put in it. I decided to make a small reform.

"Sorry. You heard what the doctor said." I finished the bottle and tossed it away. "Now we have to decide what to do about Anna."

"Do about her?"

"She murdered two people. Two more died because of the things she started. It seems to me that something ought to happen."

Anna came slowly to her knees. We faced each other.

"No one's been murdered," Pope said. "I'm all right."

"I wasn't thinking about you. Well, murder—that's a point the lawyers will have to argue. Let's see. Part of her deal with Moran was that she'd take care of the guard by drugging his coffee. Moran didn't know there was a second guard. Anna did."

"I did not," she said.

"Of course you did. That's the big thing about you, you like to keep control. Why didn't you drug Davidson, too? He's a coffee drinker. You didn't because you wanted him to kill your husband for you."

"That's a despicable lie."

I looked at Pope. "How about it, Mr. Pope? Don't you think it sounds like her?"

When he didn't answer I turned back to Anna. "You couldn't marry Dick without getting divorced. Bigamy would give Moran another hold over you. Divorce would be risky—Dick might hear about it. Your real solution was to kill Davidson. Wait a minute. To kill Moran."

My tongue was getting fuzzy, but I couldn't help it.

"You arranged the details. You knew Mrs. Pope's heart was likely to stop if somebody in a scary mask jumped out of the closet at her. And then if you didn't make it with Dick, you could always fall back on his widowed father. Right? Right. For number three, we go back to Samuel Pattberg."

"Who?" Pope said.

"The dirty movie man. He'd known Anna in the old days. She didn't want Moran to know where she was, so a killing seemed to be indicated. It was easy. She was the one sober person at the party. She saw to it that Pattberg was well supplied with bottles. Then she worked on Dick. He was feeling depressed after the movies, and something or somebody gave him the idea that he'd feel better if he burned down the building. The local fire chief, a sad son of a bitch named Minturn, found something that pointed to arson, and put in a claim for twenty thousand bucks. I've been wondering about that. If the fire wasn't Dick's idea, maybe the blackmail wasn't Minturn's. Anna was all set to spend the night with me, for diplomatic reasons, but when she heard about the missing seventy-five thousand she thought Dick must have it. She borrowed my Buick and met Chief Minturn on the highway outside of Prosper."

"How much of this do you think you can prove?" Anna asked.

"I can prove that much because you were being tailed at the time." I turned to Davidson. "Find out how this is coming over."

Davidson leaned over to speak into the radio. "Chief? Are you hearing us O.K.?"

He moved a switch, and the fire chief's voice came booming out of the loudspeaker.

"Just great!" he shouted. "But I don't want you bastards to think you can load this all on me. Let go," he said to somebody at his end of the transmission. "I can see when something's gone sour. I found the stuff at the fire, sure. But she told me what to ask for and how to do it. We were going to split it at ten apiece. She's the one who held onto the lighter, you'll notice! And if you want to know who I'm talking about, I'm talking about Anna kiss-my-ass DeLong! You can have your goddam money back, but you'd better forget it ever happened, or she's going right along with me, to the ladies' jail."

I made a twisting sign, and Davidson put the switch back in sending position.

"Do you believe any of this?" Anna said to Pope.

He looked at her for what seemed to me, in my weakened state, a long time.

"I think so," he said finally. "As Gates said, it sounds like you."

"All right!" she cried. "You thought you talked me into leaving Leo, didn't you? It wasn't like that at all. He threw me out. I was getting old, and he had another girl lined up."

"I see," Pope said. "And out of habit, you black-mailed Dick?"

"I couldn't let things just drag on and on! You promised me Mrs. Pope wouldn't last six months, and if I hadn't done something about it she would have buried us all. Gates is trying to make you think I'm some sort of a mastermind, but a lot of things happened I didn't plan. I didn't plan the robbery so Leo would be shot. That occurred to me at the very last minute, when I was fixing coffee for Davidson. I poured it out. I didn't know Dick would leave his personal signature strewn around for the firemen to find. The way he did it, he stuffed cotton in the neck of a brandy bottle, set it on fire and threw it through a window. And then he was so excited that he left the cork and the rest of the cotton on the ground beside a cigarette lighter with his initials on it. Positively brilliant! I'd had a lot of promises from people, but very little actual money, and here was a chance to make ten thousand in cash. I didn't know you wouldn't give it to him. You'd never turned him down before."

"Gates said four people died," Pope said. "I only count three."

Nobody wanted to answer him, including me. But I decided it was probably one of the things I was being paid for.

"Dick went into the fire to pull you out," I said. "He's still in there."

"How can you blame me for—" Anna cried.

Pope's eyes closed, and the lines of his face fell into a mask of such real suffering that Anna said softly, "I didn't want it to be like this. Everything I touch seems to turn to—nastiness. There must be something wrong with me, terribly wrong."

I saw no point in disagreeing with her. She took out her .25 automatic and looked down the barrel.

Pope's eyes had opened, and they widened as he saw the gun. "Gates! Take it away from her."

"She can't shoot herself with it," I said. "I took out the hammer spring last night."

This seemed to be the worst shock Anna had had yet. "I don't believe you!"

She could have made sure by putting it in her mouth, but she did it an easier way. She pushed it against my chest and pulled the trigger. Luckily I was telling the truth.

She yelled and threw the gun in my face. It whirled

end over end and the base plate struck me between the eyes. For an instant I thought that I was going to be leaving in a stretcher, after all. She dived at me. Davidson dragged her off. She went on struggling until he lifted her clear of the ground.

There was silence for a moment. Pope said quietly, "Dick went into the fire after me?"

That seemed to make all the difference. By using my last strength, I managed to keep from saying that the only reason Dick had had the chance to try to rescue his father was that he had left him unconscious on the bedroom floor, and had then started the fire himself. Pope probably needed all the comfort he could get. But I was feeling rather put upon, and I picked through Anna's purse till I found the $7500 check.

"Now I won't have to send you a bill. Saves paperwork."

When Davidson let Anna down she threw herself full-length on the grass beside the stretcher, sobbing. Most of the pins were out of her hair.

Pope turned on his elbow. After a moment he reached out to touch her loosened hair, but drew his hand back.

"Anna," he said in a voice I hadn't heard him use before. "How much of that will stand up in court? Very, very little. Listen to me! He tricked you into saying things you didn't mean. Don't worry about—" He rolled back. "Turn off that radio."

When I nodded, Davidson snapped it off.

Anna was still sobbing, but she was also listening. So was I. I am always interested in the peculiarities of human behavior.

"Don't worry about this clown, the fire chief," Pope said. "I know him. If we can't get out of it any other way, let him keep the ten thousand. We'll get a good lawyer. What can they charge you with? Drugging one detective and not drugging another? Setting a fire? Dick set the fires. Knowing somebody had a bad heart and somebody else was shut up in a projection booth? All very flimsy. Blackmail? But am I complaining about being blackmailed?"

He wasn't a bad salesman; at least he made her stop crying. She was still lying face down, and it should be remembered that I had worn her skirt into the fire. Pope patted her where he might have patted a high-strung horse.

"So it's going to be all right," he said cheerfully.

"I probably shouldn't butt in," I said. "What makes you think you can trust her?"

He looked at me, and he really seemed to be giving it some thought. "But I don't intend to marry her."

Anna raised her head and the oddly assorted pair looked at each other. I don't know what passed between them, but it seemed to be satisfactory.

I stood up, not without difficulty. The intern came forward cautiously.

"Can I put him in now, officer?"

"Yeah, take him away."

He called another attendant and they lifted Pope

into the ambulance. Anna dropped her useless automatic into her purse and took out a comb and lipstick, to put herself back together. She smoothed the nylon over her hips. Her tongue appeared briefly as she looked at me.

In a low voice, so Pope wouldn't hear, she said, "Do you want your raincoat?"

"Mail it," I said.

She looked surprised. "I thought you might—"

"I might what?"

She bit her lip, and though she had combed less than half of her hair, she turned and climbed into the ambulance.

Davidson picked up the radio. We started toward the fire, which was still burning hard.

"This isn't the Ben Gates I thought I knew," he said. "Pope's going to spend a few days in the hospital. You could pick up that raincoat in person."

I was feeling very tired and second-hand. "Irving, I don't think the law will bother with that girl at all. They might have had a case on Pattberg, but the only witness was Dick, and he's no longer around. So what the hell? I have to punish her some way."

Shelley came out of the station wagon as we approached. "Do you want to drive in now and get the money?"

"I'm sending Elmer with you," I said. "Give it to him."

I walked on. She fell in beside me, going sideways.

"We could have dinner together. I'm not busy. There's still some bourbon."

"Ask Elmer," I said, "but I doubt if he'll be interested. He doesn't go out much."

"I didn't do anything so awful, did I? I'm giving it back!"

"You're giving it back because you have to give it back."

She stood still and Davidson and I went on walking. Davidson said, "You're getting to be a moralist, Ben. Where are we going?"

"I'm looking for a girl named Hilda Faltermeier, who hasn't done anything to be ashamed of except give me a bad cup of coffee, and she didn't know it was loaded. She also used to admire my eyebrows."

If I hadn't been feeling bad enough already, a small man with a mustache seized my hand. This was Hamilton, the insurance man who had been so lofty with me when I was waking up in the Popes' library.

"Ben, this was absolutely tops. I always said you were the number-one man in New York."

"That's what you always said?"

"Now don't disappoint me, Ben. I was mistaken. I'll admit it freely. From now on I'll be singing your praises. I was with Lieutenant Minturn at the other end of the two-way. I heard the whole thing."

"So I get the retainers back?"

"You get more than the retainers. This fire isn't going to cost us a penny. Thanks to you we have a stenographic record of the policy-holder admitting it was set by his son. We'll get a reimbursement on the recreation building, and I can promise you fifteen percent of that. This was detective work at its best."

In his enthusiasm at saving his company some money, he made the mistake of slapping me on the back. It set me coughing again. I brushed at him feebly while he went on clapping me between the shoulderblades. Tears were streaming down my face.

Then Al was beside me, holding out an open pint. "We had another emergency bottle, Gates. Go easy on this one."

After I stopped coughing, I joined the Prosper volunteers and we watched the fire. When our emergency supply of whiskey was exhausted, we sent for more, in case other firemen should be overcome.

Just after dark it began to rain. That helped the firefighters, but I was the only man there without a raincoat. Something, I couldn't remember what, had happened to mine. A thoughtful member of the ladies' auxiliary let me get in the back of the station wagon. I thought it was Hilda, though the fire had died down and I couldn't be positive in the dark. It bothered me. The next morning, one of the first things I did after I woke up in a strange bed in an unfamiliar room was to look at the girl beside me.

And sure enough, it was Hilda.